# Falling Backwards

# Falling Backwards

## James Eke

A RIVERRUN
NEW FICTION BOOK

Ekstasis  Editions

National Library of Canada Cataloguing in Publication Data

Eke, James
    Falling backwards


ISBN 1-896860-98-2

    I. Title.
PS8559.K34F34 2002      C813'.6      C2002-911168-1
PR9199.4.E43F34 2002

© James Eke 2002.
Cover Art: Noreen Tomlinson

Acknowledgments: The author wishes to thank Richard Olafson and Ekstasis Editions, "John Baker" and Victoria Eke for their support. None of this would have happened without you. http://jameseke.tripod.com

Published in 2002 by:
Ekstasis Editions Canada Ltd.
Box 8474, Main Postal Outlet
Victoria, B.C. V8W 3S1

Ekstasis Editions
Box 571
Banff, Alberta T0L 0C0

THE CANADA COUNCIL | LE CONSEIL DES ARTS
FOR THE ARTS | DU CANADA
SINCE 1957 | DEPUIS 1957

BRITISH
COLUMBIA
ARTS COUNCIL
Supported by the Province of British Columbia

*Falling Backwards* has been published with the assistance of a grant from the Canada Council and the Cultural Services Branch of British Columbia.

# Grasping

angling on the sheer face of the crag I felt sweetly at peace. It was a strange, cool calmness. Not the television-engineered, skipping through a field of daisies with fantasy-perfect-blond-dancing-children kind of joys. This was real—real like the cold steel truth of a gun in the hand.

Reality now.

And it had to be that way. Rockclimbing is one of those few things in life that we can do where the rest of the world holds no sway. When you climb, the rules of the regular world start to fade into the outskirts of the mind. Climbing is pure anarchy—you're doing what most would think foolish, dangerous and apart from the regular mindset and rules of society. Climbing is a very personal, very spiritual thing that only another climber who has made it up high by their own hands and will power can ever truly understand.

There are plenty of people who think climbing and climbers are insane but the truth is that climbing rock is one of the most sane things a resident of an insane world can do to find out what it really means to be alive.

I looked down far below, seeing Squamish—like small child's toys set up in the shape of a village. It would be simple to be lulled into thinking this was all some altered reality if it weren't for the cars driving way down there—and the death grip of my hands on the rock.

The sun shining above was reflecting off small pieces of quartz making them glisten and shine like The Chief was some sort of precious gem—and in a way it was.

Voices were echoing up the rock, coming from those who'd pulled to the side of the road wondering aloud, "how'd they get up there?" and of course, "how do they get back down?" But really, the question is always more accurately, "why?"

With the sun and the wind and the feeling of the rock in the palm of my hand, it was a special day, one of those rare occasions when you could hear that special ringing tone bouncing its way up the rock from someone being turned on to something bigger than themselves.

But even then, just as the heroin junkie will say, "you'll never really get it unless you try." And the simple truth is that no one can understand until they're up top, after fighting every inch of their way and looking back down.

That fine line between heartbeats of what is life and what is death becomes more clear. The illusion is gone. Hollywood, the boss, taxes and all the other mundane minutia of our lives stay on the ground, and, even if for a short time, you climb up above it all. There's only a thin rope, a massive monolith of rock and hundreds of thousands of years of genetic programming giving the only instructions that matter—hold on, breathe, climb and relax. Nothing else matters. There is nothing else—only you and the rock.

For me, spending a day out climbing was like therapy, a chance to get away and just do what was natural.

There are those who get caught up in the whole climbing thing but not me, I just loved getting out and doing it.

I've always found it amazing that there is always a place to latch onto with a couple fingers or a well placed foot. It's as if God put mountains here for exactly this purpose—to climb them—and in climbing you come closer than ever to His face.

There are times when climbing can be just like putting on an old familiar pair of gloves. It just feels right.

A bird flew above, looking down with that same look in its eye that the people down below likely had. Or maybe I was just thinking too much instead of doing what I should have been doing—looking for the next hold.

Shaking the cobwebs out of my head I looked back up at the climb going on above me, that I was supposed to be the fall protection for.

I've heard of climbers who get hypnotised by the rock, stare at their hands, bleeding and mashed as they strain to get just a little higher. And then there are those who become transfixed by the formation of the rock or the vista around them.

My mind was drifting again, thinking about something an old-time climber had said to me about this strange pastime, in that mystical Tao-of-climbing mindset. He said that the best way to see the crag is through the eyes of a warrior—with that samurai idea of zanshin, full battlefield awareness.

While at the time I can remember thinking the old man was a couple beers short of a good time, he told me about something written by a Zen monk who explained to his samurai friend that awareness should be like looking at a huge tree—we take it all in and see it as it is. What we don't do is become transfixed by a single leaf.

Attacking a mountain is the same thing as watching that tree. You can't dwell on the small things. It was exactly what that ancient monk had mumbled about back somewhere in the dusts of time. And climbing a mountain can lead to that same sort of natural Zen bringing you to a totally different level—get hung up on any single thing and you may be falling when you should have just kept climbing.

Like being hit by a two-by-four, for some reason it all made sense now.

I looked at my hands, rock and dirt smudged. The rock had cut razor-perfect incisions in a few places. They felt sore but more alive than I could remember them ever feeling before.

Suddenly I felt as if I was watching myself climbing from somewhere in the distance. I could see my own life, which at times seemed to be more like a bad dream come true. I saw the job I felt like a slave in, bound in a lifetime of servitude. I saw my wife who seemed to be more interested in the idea of being married than the actual day to day work of it. I saw every exhausting, soul crushing piece of the disjointed puzzle my life had become— and none of it seemed right. And then, as quickly as it all started, I was back inside my head again, clinging to the rockface.

The air around me seemed to be alive with energy, every colour seemed brighter than possible. In that instant I knew why man has scaled mountains for thousands of years in search of greater truth. It was out there, dangling with the moss and little pieces of grass that somehow make their way into a crevice and creep to life. Everything seemed to make sense—that life in its infinite sadness and tragic shortness was actually pretty simple: find happiness, find meaning and live.

So I sat there, clinging to the wall suddenly seeing things with a clear light of understanding in the simple, haunting words that echoed through my head, "people too often see only the leaves on the tree, masks hiding the true self behind."

I looked at my hand again, white from the rock, bleeding in small spots, skin broken and raw.

"Nobody really sees—they just walk through life blind. What is true is right now, that if I undo my harness and step back I'm going to intimately understand the feeling of flying backwards and I'll understand why God made these perfect hand-holds—so we could hold onto death itself and climb up to...something," I mumbled to myself only realizing what I was saying when Phil my climbing buddy shouted down at me from above.

"Don't start talking to yourself—pay attention to me, if you don't mind!" he said.

"Sorry."

I looked back up at Phil climbing ahead, oblivious to the fireworks that had just ignited in my brain. My head was swimming with thoughts, thankfully I was strapped into the rock or I would have fallen.

# Images

The ferry trip back to the Sunshine Coast was...odd, as Phil kept reminding me.

"What happened to you? Some rock pelt you in the head or something?"

I just smiled and waved him off saying nothing, realizing there wasn't anything I could say that would make him understand. My insight was one of those rare moments of union with something greater. Something that would seem trivial if talked about. Phil was a great guy but if I told him I had an enlightening experience while off in some daydream it would likely be the last time we ever climbed together. But strangely, it didn't matter.

Looking around at all the people trying to make themselves busy on the ferry I couldn't help but want to stand up on my seat and shout out that there is something they were all missing. But I couldn't. Just as that old billy-goat climber had tried to teach me something that I wasn't ready for, it could only fall on deaf ears.

So instead I said nothing, smiled, joked around and felt like I was committing a crime for doing so.

By the time we got back it was dark and after a day of climbing I was tired. I thanked Phil for the climb and the drive, and went into my dark house.

Without turning a light on I wandered around our cute rental home, dropping my gear behind me.

I could hear Mary gently snoring in our room, echoing through the darkness.

Standing there, I wished there was a way I could communicate to someone about what I'd just found on the side of that mountain, place a piece of this knowledge into another human mind. I felt alone.

Wiping a tear from my cheek, I went to the bedroom and fell almost instantly asleep.

There were no dreams that I can remember, only blackness of the void but as can happen in those hollow moments between heartbeats, all was changing. And as I slept, cells renewing, skin shedding, hair growing, more evolution was in progress under the current that I would never be able to clue in on.

I'm not quite sure how long I snoozed in the darkness but at some point I woke up screaming. Looking at the clock it said I'd only been asleep for a short while. Sweat rolled down my face and through the middle of my back. My heart felt like it wanted to burst out of my chest.

As I sat there in bed, head beating with rabid thoughts I wasn't sure if I was having a dream, a vision or some distant memory—but it felt real. While my dream was jet black emptiness I sat up with terrifying images of people and places I knew rattling with speed and clarity into view in front of me. I saw fire and felt the pain of my friends from the small town of Salmon Arm where I grew up. It was terrifying to be sleeping in a sea of sheer blackness and be ripped away into a chaotic storm of faces.

These weren't the placid postcard images most people see of the peaceful bay with the arms of sloped mountains embracing it. These were chaotic visions of apocalyptic fire, frantic images of my friends battling a blaze burning down the town.

Bizarre as it seemed I felt a pang of guilt, leftover residue of the dream—or maybe more based on subconscious reality.

Mary and I had only been on the Sunshine Coast for about a year, moving down for a job that was too good to say no to. It was a tough thing to do but it felt right. Right except for the overwhelming feelings of guilt and loneliness. I felt a sense of loss, like I'd lost a good friend, or the childhood feeling of needing to be held by a parent.

But now I had a new job, and a new town. Everything was supposed to be great, only it wasn't. And with every day that passed, the thought of living or dying in this place seemed worse than a prison sentence. I knew I was bringing these feelings into every aspect of my life but was unable to pull back from the void I was falling into—a void that even my wife wasn't immune to. The thought of being with her the rest of my life filled me with a foreboding that literally made my skin crawl any time I thought about it too much.

This dream with its fire, terror and blackness reflected everything inside of me.

I once heard of a man who stood watching his child drowning in a fast moving river, unable to do a thing. One moment he could hear his child's screams and the next, only the roar of the whitewater. This dream was very similar.

As I sat there in bed, a bead of sweat rolling down my back, shivering, Mary rolled over. She reached out almost instinctively knowing where I was in the dark.

"Are you all right hon?" her voice came out with a little early morning gravel.

"Just a bad dream."

"You've been having lots of those lately."

"Yeah…this one the guys in Salmon Arm were dying, running crazy with fire all around them—just their faces up close screaming," I nodded, unable to remember what other dreams she was talking about.

"It's over now," she said running her hand down my chest. "Just go back to sleep and forget all about it."

What more could she say. But the simple truth was that I couldn't just forget about it—even if it was just a dream—it was real. Or at least real enough.

I put my head back on the pillow and turned towards her. The familiar, warm smell of her hair made me feel safe, and a feeling that nothing else in the world mattered. As I drifted off I realized I could still feel the presence of the mountain, the rock under my hand, and the open air around me—and it felt good.

# Deja Vu

The next morning started like any other but finished quite differently.

I went through my usual ritual—up, the obligatory trip to the can, out for a jog.

It was while out on this bizarre daily chore that I decided suddenly and with a calm finality to just keep running.

There are moments in life when you just know you're at a fork in the road—you can turn either way but you can't turn back. If you're lucky, these moments come with clarity and you realize fully what is happening. You may not know why or how or what is going to happen next but if you step into this new light with purpose, your life is never the same afterwards.

I knew I was a bastard for what I was doing—leaving a beautiful wife—and I knew that everyone would think I blew a few rivets. But I ran. Fast—faster than I'd ever run before.

And for the first time in years my body wasn't screaming out to stop running as it usually did on these knee pounding attempts at keeping death at bay. Everything inside of me kept pushing me forward, yelling from every cell, "faster...faster."

I looked into the cars and deep into the eyes of the faces of the drone drivers, grey and unmoving in their metal coffins on their way to yet another day in 45 years of work to eventually be told to pack their things and get out.

I was running with a maniac grin—my heart was pounding in my chest, trying to break out—but I was free. Everything seemed clear. I knew where I was going and I'd run all the way and never stop if need be.

Call me crazy, but what I was doing made a lot of sense— more than what the long line of cars on the way to catch the early morning ferry to another day in the packaged offices in Vancouver were doing. Or at least it did to me.

The mad sprint was the single most sane thing I think I'd ever done in my life.

I thought back to the day before, clinging to the side of that mountain, looking out below and my sudden moment of understanding. Everything was so clear now—even more clear than the day before.

I thought of the view of those cars driving back and forth beneath that cold rock that would be there long after all of them were reduced to dust.

With these memories spurring me on, I sprinted leaving a loving wife behind. I sprinted past mournful, crawling traffic. I sprinted, steaming, kicking up dust—leaving my new home on the beautiful Sunshine Coast behind with its paradise-on-earth beaches, trees and eagles.

I sprinted out of my entire life, running towards a light— and I ran with a face sore from smiling, enjoying every joint-jarring bound of it.

# Passage

Of course I had no money on me, so by the time I'd managed to run the half-marathon to the Langdale ferry terminal I realized something had better happen soon or I'd have to do some pretty good explaining to either the police—who Mary would likely have called by this time worried I was road-kill—or to Mary herself.

So instead of coming up with a good answer to the question of "what now" I stood in one spot, shuffling my feet (I didn't actually notice the foot shuffle until some small kid walked by staring at my dusty shoes).

I stopped and looked at the group of people who were waiting to walk onto the ferry.

As the ferry workers lifted the gate and waved the people aboard I looked back over my shoulder—I half expected something or someone to grab my shoulder and tell me to get back home. But it didn't happen.

Instead I decided to get my legs (which felt more like rubber bands after the long run they'd just made) moving and walk on board the ferry bound for Vancouver.

No one seemed to notice me, despite the fact I was red-faced and soaked with sweat. I thought to myself that I really must be on a mission from God.

In all my life I'd never even tasted a sample out of a bulk

food bin before but somehow I became invisible right then and there. I didn't notice it at first but everything started to show itself.

"Great day isn't it?" I said to a young blond woman with perky 20-something breasts shown off proudly through a white muscle shirt which also revealed a delicious-looking pierced navel.

I saw a half grin, so I knew she heard me—though she could just have easily been smiling at a thought she'd just had—but proving my point she just continued up the stairs to the passenger deck. I stood there on the steps for a moment, watching her hips swaying back and forth as she climbed the last few stairs.

"If I haven't become invisible, I'm at least translucent," I said out loud to myself as an elderly couple pushed their way past me not even giving me a sideways glance.

Once on the main passenger deck, I purposefully headed toward couples walking together and groups engaged in deep conversation. All just went around and by me without a pause.

Finally I decided to rest my sore feet on the upper deck's forward smoking area. To further my experiment—or maybe just to entertain myself a little—I sat a few inches away from an attractive university student who was far too cute to be smoking. She wasn't even inhaling. With "UBC" flashed with pride across her chest, clutching a sociology text with her free hand I figured she'd make the perfect candidate for another test subject.

Her eyes didn't even move from the book.

"Don't even bother—she can't see you or won't see you," a voice called out.

I looked around.

"Over here man...don't you get it—none of their type is going to see you—they don't see true faces anyway." The voice was coming from a bearded face, inside a hooded army jacket.

I walked over to the scruffy-looking bum. And "bum" is a good word to describe him. He smelled bad—a combination of pot, urine and something rotten. My bet was that if black teeth could emit an odour, that was where this one started.

"So why can you see me?" I asked not even noticing that as soon as I stood up the young student had grabbed her things and disappeared herself.

"Because I have the eyes to see brother—you need to have the eyes to see."

I sat down with a thump beside him, telling myself I didn't really mind the stench too much—truth was, I imagined I smelled pretty rank myself.

# Vision

We sat together for the rest of the trip—most of the time not speaking, just sitting, looking out over the water.

At one point a sudden bout of shivers set in, my body shaking violently. Mojo, as he said people called him, took off his coat and threw it on top of me.

If I thought he smelled bad, I entered a whole different dimension of odour inside that old army jacket. But at least the shaking subsided.

I could see the pock mark scar badges of a junkie running up his arms. It explained a lot—but at the same time opened a new door to a room full of questions.

"So why were you on the Sunshine Coast? I asked him looking though his long matted hair and beard.

"I like to go there and hide out in the jungle and just get my shit together. Everyone needs a break...you know what I mean?"

I just nodded.

We hit another pocket of silence, one of those uncomfortable zones where you can't think of a single thing to talk about but don't really want to wander away either.

Eventually, as we sat watching Howe Sound pass us, Mojo broke the silence. "Where are you going—or do you have any idea?"

"What do you mean?"

He grinned under his beard. "People don't have that look on their face if they're on their way to a meeting. They don't jump onto a ferry to the city without a bag or at least a pair of pants."

I looked down at my hands remembering something I read in school in one of Shakespeare's plays—the words "out damn spot," rang though my head. While there wasn't anything on them, my hands felt dirty—rotten.

"You know, I haven't really thought about it. I just went to the ferry and I got on."

"No bag, no clothes, no money—you really did leap before you looked."

We both laughed. I wanted to tell him I had identification in my fanny pack but he was right—no cash.

"I guess you're right—it wasn't something I planned, it just kind of exploded around me."

Mojo nodded his head, clumps of matted hair flopping around.

"So what are your plans then?"

Shrugging my shoulders and glancing back at the scars on his arms, I half-mumbled, "...don't really have any."

And for the first time since I started running it suddenly dawned on me that I really did turn a corner in my life. I was on the run with nowhere to go, and no money to get there. But it strangely didn't scare me—the idea of being on the run kind of excited me.

"Well, why don't you just hang out with me for awhile. At least until you get a few things figured out," he said lighting up the butt of a tattered and bent cigarette he pulled from a zip-lock baggie filled with similar smokes.

I nodded and leaned back pulling the stinking jacket around me tighter and thought to myself that I was actually feeling better than I had in a long time—like a big weight that had been pulling me down for most of my life had recently been lifted—I felt taller and stronger. And even though I didn't have anything I was sure I'd do just fine.

"Sure...that sounds great."

# First Steps

While I felt confident enough about being invisible that I could hop a bus without paying once we stepped off the ferry, Mojo said bus drivers were notorious for being able to see the translucent. He decided we'd walk.

"Everyone else in the world might pass you by but bus drivers, cops and guard dogs have an uncanny knack of noticing even the most invisible."

I smiled and walked beside him, following to wherever it was we were going.

We must have been quite a sight—a long haired, dirty and smelly vagrant walking and talking to some strange looking, shorts and t-shirt clad jogger. Or was I a runner?

I hardly noticed most of the walk from Horseshoe Bay through West Vancouver to the Lions Gate bridge. Mojo kept us deep in conversation about a multitude of different topics and observations—he was a master of spontaneous conversation. Not once did he even start talking about the usual mundane topic of weather.

It was only when midway over the Lions Gate bridge that I noticed how far we'd actually walked.

I looked back towards where the ferry terminal would have been if I could have seen it.

"How long have we been walking?"

"Dunno," Mojo said walking on ahead. "Doesn't really matter to me to be honest, we've got to get where we're going and this is the way we're headed."

"What time is it?" I yelled at his back, pausing to peer over the railing on the bridge.

"I don't know and I don't really care—what's with all the questions man? Do I look to you like someone who has a business meeting to get to?" he glared at me over his shoulder.

"No, I was just..." I didn't really know what I was asking—or why.

Boats passed below us. For a moment I fantasized about what it would be like to jump. Would the fall kill me? What would it feel like crashing into the water after what had to be at least a few seconds of free fall. The creeping feeling of vertigo made its way up my legs. I leaned over the edge a little further—I couldn't help but think about all those people who had told me that anyone who jumps from any great height is dead before impact—part of me just wanted to know the truth.

I shook my head. "That is a far way down but you'd still be alive when you hit," I said out loud but talking only to myself. Who wanted to think of the terror and sudden realization that snapped through a person's mind at warp speed after the jump?—it was child logic to think anything but the reality.

My knuckles turned white gripping the rail and my legs felt like they were made of water and about to collapse.

I looked at Mojo shuffling ahead, West Vancouver to my right and the water far below. Nothing much more to do than continue, one step after the next to whatever was waiting for me on the other side of the bridge.

"Hey Mojo!"

He turned with a half-glance and continued his way across the bridge that shook with every vehicle zipping past us.

My legs were getting very tired—and well they should be, I thought over and over to myself. But managed to haul them more through willpower than endurance.

Finally catching up to him he looked over at me through his jungle of hair. "What were you doing back there?"

"I don't know, just looking—taking in everything—where we'd come from and where we're going...where are we going?"

"Nowhere—but first we have to make a stop in the park."

"For what?"

"You ask too many questions...either come or don't."

I knew Mojo wasn't used to company and to be honest I was probably driving him nuts but for whatever reason, he wanted to keep an eye on me—or so he was letting on.

With cars whizzing past we made it over the bridge, past the giant lion statues that stand silently guarding the old landmark and into the welcoming forest.

# Into the Green

Vancouver's Stanley Park has always been a magical place for me. I have vivid pictures in my mind, images of going there as a child with my parents during our trips to the cleaner part of the big city—it was always great. Food from the vendors in the park, beachcombing for lost treasures around the shore and all the neat people wandering around with big smiles on their faces.

Before moving to Salmon Arm, my family lived in East Vancouver's grey. I can remember gathering up a bag full of toys and other gear and we'd hop a bus, ending up in the lush green of the park—massive trees and wildlife within the loud and busy city. It was an amazing thing for a boy used to playing in paved streets and sidewalks. When I wasn't in Stanley Park it was easy to forget there was more green in the world than our small well trimmed square of lawn in the back of our home.

But as I flashed back to happier times, Mojo didn't seem to have plans on slowing down to smell the roses. And he didn't seem to have any desire to stick to any of the trails and paths through the park that most people choose to walk on.

I tried my best to stay a few steps behind him as he dodged through the bush but he'd been on this thin goat trail—if it was a trail of any sort—some time before, or at least he did a good job at looking like he knew where he was headed. While I was concentrating as hard as I could on not losing an eye on one of the branches that snapped back in his wake, he moved through the brambles and bushes with ninja-like ease.

"Where are you taking me?" I yelled ahead but to no answer. I wondered to myself if he even knew I was behind him.

Suddenly we came to a clearing—of sorts. I was just about to open my mouth again and say something about wishing he'd slow down a notch, or how glad I was to be in a clearing—then I noticed all the men around us.

I'd heard people talk before about these secluded pockets in the massive forest park before. The stories all said that there were places gay men met to do their thing, where satanists or witches met and the wooded lairs of junkies. Up until now I thought it was all just some exaggerated urban legend about a park that is more woods than trail.

It was a very uneasy feeling walking into this group. Time seemed to suddenly shift into slow motion. Heads turned slowly, all with eyes focused on us—it made me feel naked, and naked wasn't exactly how I wanted to feel at the moment.

I looked at Mojo's back wondering why he'd brought me here and dreading the answer. But just as I was about to open my mouth, or turn my back to run the way I came, he turned to me grinning and waved his hand, whispering, "come on, I don't think this is where we're going—keep moving and don't look so damned scared."

My heart lifted at those simple words and his grin. With all their eyes still on us and the forest suddenly sounding very quiet we made our way through without stopping—or looking back.

# Free

The words come without breaking a tooth though I'm not proud of them—shooting up for the first time came remarkably easy.

Mojo finally stopped his shuffle through the woods in another clearing, this one empty except for old blankets and cardboard scattered around and a couple people passed out under bushes. And by the used syringes at our feet littered in small piles almost everywhere I knew full well why we were there.

Moving over to a relatively clean spot under a Douglas Fir tree, Mojo motioned for me to hunker down beside him.

Without a word he opened his bag and went to work.

I tried not to watch and even started to tell him about my lifelong hero, St. Joseph of Copertino, "...he was born in 1603...he could levitate...or fly, and did it in front of reputable people and it is all documented—he was really dumb but he's the patron saint of students."

Mojo wasn't listening, busy pulling his belt tightly around his arm with his teeth. I watched his veins enlarge as I continued to talk about St. Joseph.

"He is recorded as having flown the furthest backwards...the church treated him like a freak though, told him to stay away from the public...kind of sad actually."

He plunged the heroin filled needle deep into the blue-green vein, letting his jaw loosen the grip of the belt. I could see an instant slump in his frame.

As I watched he set the needle up again.

Noticing that my mouth was actually hanging open, I closed it and looked back at his arm. A small drop of blood ran down his skin from where he'd injected himself with the precision of a surgeon.

"What are you waiting for?"

"What do you mean?" I said looking at him as he lifted his arm, handing me the now fully loaded needle.

"You can't just hang out here. Or are you just going to bail on me?"

I didn't quite know what to say. While I was far from as pure as driven snow I would freely admit shooting up heroin in the middle of the woods with people passed out on cardboard 20 feet away wasn't something I thought I'd do when I woke up in the morning—or any other time.

"I just haven't done anything like this before." I heard myself almost from a distance, while rolling my sleeve up to the shoulder. Everything else that followed felt the same, as if I was watching some stranger from a few feet away doing something that horrified and excited me at the same time.

As soon as the heroin hit I could understand why people become junkies. To me it felt like a prolonged orgasm or the feeling Buddhist monks must get after prolonged meditation that hooks them enough to keep them in a temple.

It crashed over me like a wave, leaving me in its wake like a dreamer in a dream. I didn't care about the fact I was lying on a mouldy piece of cardboard—I didn't care about anything. And it felt good.

When the wave finally washed back early the next morning I was alone.

Mojo had at least been kind enough to leave me his coat and a note saying "see ya later." Of course it didn't say where or when.

I can't say I really minded.

I was cold and damp and felt like shit, my head was swimming.

Hoisting myself up I looked around—the woods seemed much quieter than they had the day before.

My arm ached, and a big yellow and purple bruise screamed out as the remaining evidence of what I'd done. I shook my head.

Mojo's coat seemed to stink even worse than it had yesterday. When I first threw it on I was hit with the hammer of nausea and as I could see by the puke around me it wasn't the first time I'd felt like that after lying down on the old box with Mojo.

But instead of letting go, I managed to get myself to my feet and started back the way I had come—or at least what I could remember still feeling half stoned.

After wandering around in the woods I made my way to the Lost Lagoon—I've always loved wandering around that stagnate water.

Watching a huge swan float past me I couldn't help but remember the last time I'd been in the park with Mary a few months earlier.

The swan made its way past me and joined a group of other birds.

Grabbing the back of a bench I lowered myself down, put my hands over my face and cried tears that surprized me with their sudden attack out of nowhere. Through my tears I noticed the old retired lap-dog walkers making wide detours around me.

Mary's face seemed to be reflected in each tear as I wiped them away. I cried for the sorrow and heartbreak I must be causing her. It seemed unreal that I was doing what I was doing—but at the same time, as cruel as it felt, I was glad to be gone.

I wanted to call her, let her know I was all right but I just couldn't. Sometimes going on into darkness is easier than turning to face the light.

As I stood up and wandered away from the park I rubbed my face with the filthy sleeve of Mojo's coat and told myself that I could never go back—so much had changed already.

And I had a feeling this was just the beginning.

# Reflections

Wandering around downtown Vancouver is a very lonely thing for me. As long as I can remember that's the way it has made me feel. It doesn't matter if I'm in a crowd of people, with friends, or just by myself—the feeling is always the same—emptiness.

I've seen people hurt, begging, bleeding, lost and broken—all bring the same general response from the moving wave of the sidewalk crowd. Nothing. And I felt the same.

Sure, there is the occasional person who stops or the child or two who stares with wide eyes, clutching tightly to its mother. But these are usually rare reactions. For the most part the wave travels on with only periodic sideways stares. It's probably the same in most big cities around the world. Everyone looks out for themselves and anyone willing to get in their way is simply side-stepped.

The sidewalk moves with empty eyes staring ahead into the nothingness of the city.

But strangely, I think it is this feeling of mass, organized despair and mutual avoidance that makes the downtown such a magnet. You can get lost with a group of people. Even with the packed, flowing sidewalk—you are just one of the many, communally humming along, wandering to no place in general.

And that was just where I was headed—no place in general.

And I was looking forward to getting there, while wondering how I'd know if I'd reached it when I arrived.

The usual crowd was already hanging out, milling around the art gallery. I stood there, then I sat there, huddling under Mojo's filth infested coat, watching some unemployed genius playing a handful of chess games against a few different people at the same time. Musicians bongoed and strummed, writers wrote, some teenage boys came by for a little while whistling at women as they passed. And a few people did just what I was doing—sat or stood—doing nothing.

Eventually someone who felt I must be doing myself harm in some way—as if sitting and standing in shorts and a smelly jacket can be bad for your health—decided to give me exact directions (even scribbling them on a pad of note paper taken from a briefcase) on how to get to the "street drop-in," as this concerned individual called it, stressing the name like it was an approaching storm.

I mused to myself that I had been here only one day and I was already considered "street."

I don't think I said two words, just nodding along with something about, "Jesus wanting more for me." I smiled and shrugged a promise I'd drop by the centre. God knows I needed to find a meal, some clothes and a place to crash. There was no way I was going to hike back into the bush to find "Junkie Town" again. My arm ached just thinking about last night.

As it turned out, "the centre" as they called it, was painless enough and I wasn't invisible, or even translucent—instead I was treated a little too kindly. The people there (church workers, missionary types) smiled too much and the coffee tasted more like water with brown colouring—but it was warm.

And despite the smiles that looked painful on their faces and almost as painful for me to watch, I managed through a small discussion about how, "there was more for me in life than sitting on the steps of the art gallery." They even set me up with some none-too-bad new clothes. Of course afterwards they sat me down again for another one-on-one rap session.

"Don't you want more from your life than heroin and a life on the streets?" a smiling young girl said to me.

"Oh, I'm not a junkie," I said covering my arm with an open palm as if she could see my bruise through the long sleeves and coat they'd given to me. "No, last night was the first time I'd ever shot up..."

She sat staring, the smile now more like a plastic Mrs. Potato Head grin.

I realized I'd already said more than I should have. The words, "cult...get out..." kept rattling around in my brain but the truth was it was warmer sitting put.

"If you aren't in trouble why have you come to us? What are you hoping to find?" she asked with a voice much older than her young face. "Aren't you lost...looking for something?"

I just stared at her not sure what to say at this point—but instead opened my mouth and told her everything.

"Two days ago everything was the way it always had been. Actually it was better—I spent the day climbing in Squamish with my friend. Then the next day I woke up, went for a jog and just kept going. I left a beautiful wife behind who is likely going insane wondering where the hell I've gotten to or if my body will ever show up." She was still staring about me.

"Then I found a junkie, we shot up. I woke up and wandered for few hours and ended up here. You probably think I'm a piece of shit and you're right."

She wasn't smiling any longer but there was still a pleasant glow about her. I smiled to myself thinking an angel would probably look something like her, not all stoic and winged.

"I don't think you are anything but the perfect person God made you and us all. We all have tests and sin. Each of us has to live the life we were given. Sometimes this means going through things we can't understand when we're in the midst of them," she finished.

I watched her chest move as she breathed silently waiting for something to happen.

I couldn't help but think to myself how much I'd love to pull off that tight sweater she was wearing, unzip that skirt and roll around naked with her right there on the floor of her small office.

I smiled to myself thinking about my sudden fantasy and how strange it is that those thoughts come through even in the most serious of times. The corners of her mouth curled in a grin—I looked at my shoes and could feel the heat of my cheeks blushing as if she'd just telepathically understood what I was thinking.

But as she sat there with an angelic look on her face, the light reflecting off her long hair making it seem like it was shining, I couldn't help but ride this train of thought.

Looking up from my shoes I saw her breasts looking perfect under her tight grey sweater, rising and falling with each breath. I blinked thinking about how I'd love to run a hand a few inches past the place where her smooth, soft legs stopped and the short, tight skirt began.

She smiled wider and glanced downward.

Sometimes it is far better to see the ripe fruit on the tree than it is to pick it. It's the same with most things in life, dreaming, lusting and silent appreciation are often better than the after-knowledge of having.

So I just smiled silently at my erotic young angelic mission-ary and felt the wise man for it.

After a few more minutes of silence, she got up and lead me

to a kitchen where I was instructed on the finer points of nutrition like I was in some sort of high school home economics class for bums.

After I'd eaten, I was taken to a place I could stay for the night—but just one night I was told. The next day I could come back in the afternoon if I wished but only if there was room. House rules.

But they were rules you could respect, after all there were a lot of people out there who needed a warm bed, a home economics class and a cute, friendly girl to smile at them, making them feel like they mattered.

As I lay down I watched her walking away, enjoying her leaving almost as much as I enjoyed her company.

The bed was warm (institutional blankets) and despite the sounds of other street people sniffling, burping and farting all night long, it was a good place to sleep—and I drifted off into pleasant dreams of somewhere else.

# Pavement

Days begin to blur together on the street.

There aren't the diversions and divisions we're conditioned to: breakfast, work, lunch, work, supper, T.V., snack, sleep and so on.

On the street it's much different, mostly because you sleep where and when you can. The best street food is usually a slice of pizza—it's cheap and has most of the food groups in it. Dumpster diving for bottles to pay for a slice doesn't take long.

With sleep and feeding messed up, routine vanishes. You begin to realize that while it gets dark and cold at night, there is no magic separation between days. Sometimes, when things are bad or some goons are out smacking around street people you stay on the move, same goes for when there just isn't anywhere good enough to sleep or it's just too cold.

All there is to remind you of the ongoing rolling of days is endlessly growing hunger, fatigue and various pains that come along for the ride. But eventually you get used to all of this too.

Day after day, night after night, you find yourself shuffling as darkness falls, around the procession of streets all with the same loneliness. Or you huddle in some long forgotten doorway trying to keep the rain off.

It's an existence that blurs reality.

And it was in this mind and consciousness altering state that days, weeks and months began to roll past in one continuous train of shivering, piss-drenched gutters, shooting up in alleyways, sometimes turning a trick for a fix, endless night.

I lost track of all time. Eventually all that showed me that time was continuing around me was that when I pulled up my sleeve I was blasted into reality with the calm clarity that I had the scarred arms of a junkie.

I was still wearing Mojo's coat (I'd passed off the one the missionaries had given to me a long time ago, though I couldn't quite remember when that was)—and it stunk a whole new world of stench.

"How long have I been here?" I said out loud.

Nothing and no one answered.

The city moved on around me, a bus rolling by followed by a stream of cars. The nicely dressed people inside didn't even notice the raggedy-looking guy holding out an arm covered in mosquito bite scars to the air, crying.

# Wandering

Even with the realization of just how fucked up I'd become—or perhaps because of it, I just kept shooting up. It dulled all the pain and reality. At some point I hooked up with a woman who always managed to fix me up with good stuff and the best part was that she did it for nothing. Most of the time.

She liked me for one reason or another and would give me some of her heroin as long as I put my dick inside her from time to time. Although she was about 20 years older than me and looked at least 30 years older, her bed was at least better to sleep in than some doorway that smelled like urine.

Her name was Gina but she called herself Ginger—never asked her why and to be honest I didn't really care. We had that kind of relationship (if you want to call it that) she could have called herself anything—we were more like each other's keepers, friends, close friends but far from in love. To be truthful I don't know if we were even deeply in like—we were just there for each other.

While she was a junkie she still managed to hold down a job as a temp.

How she became a junkie I'll never know since she demanded to be shot up with junk but wouldn't do it herself—didn't even want to look at the needle. She'd just stick out her foot, spread her toes and then let out a deep moan as the drug entered her.

Sometimes I'd just sit there and watch her lying on the bed, eyes heavy, rolling around in her head—to be honest she looked kind of sexy stoned. That's probably why I hung around. That and the supply of heroin.

While most people would think every junkie lives on the street with nothing at all, they'd be surprised to know just how many wander around them every day. They are out there walking past you on the sidewalk, next door, at work—drug addiction doesn't discriminate, it just consumes.

But soon even Ginger tired me out. Most of my days were spent sitting on a street corner, small sign in front of me scribbled in a black marker asking for money—I'd just sleep and hope to find a few more coins when I woke up. If pickings were slim I knew I could always count on Ginger, but with her there were strings attached.

Some days as I sat on the corner, head sprawled on my arms, hugging my knees, I'd daydream these fantasies that she and I were actually a couple but the truth was far from that and I was first to admit it. We rarely talked—she picked me up on the street one night with the temptation of a fix. After that it was just more of the same.

And as for the people I met day to day on the sidewalk—they weren't exactly the type that you'd invite home to meet mom. One morning when a junkie didn't wake up from the grate he was sleeping on, a swarm of people surrounded him, taking every last thing that was of any worth. This was the glamorous life of a street person.

At least with Ginger I had access to a place where I could keep myself bathed—there were plenty of people I met on the street who crawled with various other lifeforms—none nice.

So life went, one needle after another until the day I met Jo. She was a street person too but different. Jo worked for a newspaper that printed weekly editions and gave them to street people to sell. It was a great idea—one I didn't want any part of personally—but a great idea nonetheless.

For whatever reason, she decided to sell her copies on the same corner where I was hunkered down for my day of asking for alms.

"Why don't you go do that somewhere else?" I said to her looking up from behind my sign.

"Instead of sitting there looking all downtrodden why don't you get up and get some of these papers and sell them?"

I knew all about the paper she was involved in from other people I'd bumped into that were doing the same thing but I didn't have any interest—I had enough on my mind, dealing with Ginger and trying to sleep.

"Begging is begging, whether you're selling a paper or sleeping on a corner with a sign. Hell, if these suits that walk past all day had any brains they'd realize what they do isn't all that far from what we do either."

"Hey man, don't include me in your little philosophy—I'm no junkie."

"Yeah right."

She walked closer to me. She was tough looking, shaved head, tattoos on well maintained arms—not the kind of woman you'd really want to arm wrestle.

"What is that supposed to mean?"

"Why are you selling that then?"

She squatted down to eye level. "I used to be a junkie like you but I've been clean for months now—that shit will kill you—I saw too many friends checking out because of all this," she said sweeping her arm around her.

"So if you're clean why are you still down here?"

She looked down at the pavement. "It's kind of hard to get a job when you have no real skills except for knowing how to stay alive on the street—but I have plans. I want to travel or go to school. I'm still getting my shit together but it will all happen."

For the first time in what seemed like an eternity I realized I was having a conversation with someone who I could talk to. Maybe we both just needed to talk to someone.

Smiling she asked me if I'd join her for a cup of coffee, I nodded and took her hand. It felt good to have made a friend— it wasn't until I was a block away that I realized I'd forgotten my sign back on the corner. I just left it there.

# Ronin

Sitting down in the coffee shop the first good look I had of Jo was her perfectly shaven head. I'd seen other women with heads trimmed down to the skin but in her I saw the perfect head. And of course instead of a profound statement what came out of my head was stupidity.

"Guess you don't have to worry about shampoo?"

She looked up at me. For a minute I thought she was going to shove a fist down my throat but instead she smiled and grabbed my hand, gently rubbing it over her scalp.

"Everyone who sees my head for some reason asks or wants to ask if they can touch it, so enjoy."

I felt like a boy who catches his first glimpse of a naked woman—like I'd touched something important. Of course it was just a head but my eyes were wide and I smiled from ear to ear.

We sat down and my second surprise was a simple tattoo running down the side of her left arm, black inked Japanese characters.

"You like my tattoo? It says Ronin—a feudal Japanese thing meaning a wandering warrior."

I sat staring at her for a few seconds processing the new vision I suddenly had of her.

"You sure are more than you make out to be standing on the corner like that."

"What is that supposed to mean—we are all more than we seem. What we all see of each other is just projected from our own minds. There is no way we can really see what is there."

"Yeah...I mean standing out there I just never thought I'd be talking to some sort of Shaolin priest or something."

She looked down at the table, playing with a spoon.

"Hey, I don't mean to embarrass you or anything. It's cool. I mean you really have your shit together."

Jo looked up and said slowly, "none of us has our shit totally together. I got this tattoo and shave my head to remind myself of that. I guess that's why I've stayed down here too. In a way I kind of aspire to that whole Kung Fu vision of the Shaolin priest wandering around penniless, doing good, living the real life and forgetting all the rest."

We just looked at each other for a few minutes. I wanted to say something special or something at least interesting but the waitress came by with our coffee and I decided that Jo would appreciate the silence more.

Time just flew by as we sat together, Jo talking about the street Zen she'd picked up before getting hooked on junk, during and after she'd cleaned up. In her I could see the start of a whole new breed of wandering Ronin. People looking to close the door to the profane falseness that the modern world was placing on their shoulders, instead choosing a different reality where life meant much more.

She explained that she'd come to Vancouver from Montreal about two years ago expecting the West to offer gold in exchange for her efforts in getting across the country. But instead she found only one dead-end low-paying job after another. One thing had led to something else and she started using. The street wasn't a far fall.

"I'd studied the martial arts most of my life until coming out here and hoped to find some sort of enlightenment but instead what I found was more suffering until one day it all dawned on me."

"What?" I asked moving closer as if she was telling a secret.

"During a trip I had, I remembered something a Buddhist teacher had told me soon after moving here, that monks when they are first ordained are called something that translates to something like wandering or floating cloud."

"A cloud?"

"Don't you get it? A wandering or floating...shit it doesn't matter—a cloud. Look at the sky any day and you'll see clouds moving, changing, appearing and dissipating, no two seconds are they the same. And even on the darkest days when the clouds look like they are about to burst, suddenly a blue hole will appear and the sun will break on through. I decided right then that I wanted to be like that—not in a monastery but in real life. Do you know about Bodhisattvas?"

"Not really..."

"They are individuals who train hard and devote their whole being to the betterment of the universe. That's what I want to be. And part of that is being real, but always with the memory that I am to be like a cloud and even if someday I'm a storm cloud I will remember that the other side is still sunny and a beautiful blue."

There are moments in life that you wish you could carve out a piece and keep it forever and this was one of them. I just sat there with her words echoing like a chime in the wind but tickling my soul from toes up to the tip of my hairs. The air felt electric.

We sat and talked most of the day, Jo telling of her views on life and me just sucking it all up.

Employees of the joint seemed to be starting to look down at us, so we got up and walked outside. Hitting the air was like a truck running into me from behind, unseen. I remembered where I was.

"You know, I don't want to sound weird or anything but I would love to talk more about this stuff—I hear you talk and I remember a part of me that wanted to be just like you but instead look at me. I stink, and I'm totally fucked up. I don't know if I want help or just want a way out of this whole thing. But whatever it is, something has to change—I know these streets are killing me."

Jo put a hat on her head and buttoned her coat then stood looking at me. At first I thought she was just going to turn her back and walk away but instead she put her arms around me and held on tight.

"This life can be amazing if you let it be. And I will be here to help you fight every step of the way, but some battles we have to face for ourselves—the one ahead of you is a hard one. The winning or the losing is totally up to you."

My body shook but strangely no tears came out. I just stood there shaking like I was possessed by some demon and it knew I was going to try to take it out. But despite the tremors, Jo just stood where she was and held on tight.

"You can do this—I can see it in you."

Images of Mary came into my mind. Still shaking I broke free of Jo's strong grip and stood back as if suddenly remembering something. I looked at her and turned my back.

She grabbed me by the shoulder.

"What are you doing?" she said pulling me around.

"I don't know, I just have to be alone. This shit is just too much for me. I'm so confused—and who the hell are you to come out of nowhere and tell me what I should do?"

"I haven't said a word about what you should do. But hey," she said grabbing my arm and pulling up the sleeve. "If you want to think that this is what your life is all about go for it man. But I think we both know it isn't. All I'm saying is that there are people who will help you. I'll help you if you want it. But if you don't, just go back to your corner and your sign and get some more money for your next score."

She shoved a copy of the paper she had with her into my pocket. "If you decide you want my help or just want to talk, contact me through this place. I hang out there a lot and write some stuff and do odd jobs for them. It's all up to you."

Then as quickly as I met her she turned her back and walked away.

I just stood there watching her cross the street, wondering what was happening to me. Soon she was gone from sight around a corner.

# Again

Despite the great motivational conversation, less than two hours after talking to Jo I was at Ginger's place sprawled on her couch chasing the dragon. I heard every word Jo said, I agreed with her one hundred per cent but I needed the heroin to make everything feel right.

"Just because a man leaves his life behind doesn't mean he does it with immunity to emotion," I mumbled to myself as I drifted off in a haze.

When I woke up the next morning I was still on the couch but at some point Ginger (or someone) had thrown a blanket over me. The place was empty. As I got up and shuffled around the apartment I noticed that Ginger's good shoes were gone which likely meant she was out on a temp job.

I made myself something to eat and sat down at the table in the kitchen.

My coat was thrown over a chair beside me, Jo's paper sticking out of the pocket. I grabbed it and looked it over as I wolfed down some food.

It wasn't a great product by any means but it did have a special feel to it, knowing that it was put together by people trying to do something more with their lives than sitting on street corners. As I read it I slowly nodded as if I had to talk myself into going to see her. It didn't take much.

The sun was shining and the streets were clean from a late night rainstorm. You could smell that wonderful scent of rain in the air—it was a great day. I felt better than I'd felt in a long time and practically skipped down the sidewalk to the paper's office hoping to see Jo and apologise for my bizarre behaviour the day before.

When I walked into the office it was buzzing with activity, people rushing around, phones ringing. Not wanting to bother anyone I just sat down on a chair and watched.

About an hour passed before anyone said anything to me. Some nice guy came over and asked if I'd like a coffee, smiling I nodded and then after coming back with a small foam cup he disappeared back into the hive of activity.

I was just about to leave when I saw Jo come in through a back door. Like a jack-in-the-box I jumped up and waved, "hey, Jo!"

She looked over—as did a bunch of other people who seemed to suddenly realize I was there—and grinned, jerking her head back slightly as if to say, "hi, just wait a minute."

I sat back down. I could see she was busy talking with someone but soon enough she was stomping her way over.

"Didn't think I'd see you again," she said looking down at me. I didn't really notice yesterday how muscular she really was, with round shoulders, large forearms and biceps shown off with the muscle shirt she was wearing.

"I'm full of surprises."

"I'm sure you are." She folded her arms over her chest.

"I just wanted to say I was sorry for the stupid way I acted yesterday. I mean, you're really cool and I would really like to hang out or something. If you'd like to."

"You got stoned last night didn't you?"

Not quite sure if honesty really was the best policy I just

looked at her for a couple seconds.

"I'm not going to judge you if you did but you need to be straight with me. You act and talk like someone who doesn't want to be ruled by the drug but then you go and do it again—I know all about it, I know what it is like. I was there."

"Yeah, I did. I don't know if I do it because I need it or I want to dull reality or just because I'm so fucking bored most of the time."

We looked at each other, neither sure what to say next but Jo beat me to silence cracking.

"Well I tell you what—tonight my girl and I are going to this cool joint over on Commercial, there are a couple writers there doing a spoken word gig. It'll be fun and I'll keep you entertained. After you can crash at my place if you want."

She told me to meet her back at the office in a few hours and then we'd get a bite to eat and head to the bar.

As I wandered down the street to find something to do for a few hours, smiling from ear to ear the only thing that broke my happiness were the words, "...my girl and I..."

# Heroes

Just as I'd  expected to see, Jo came strolling down the street a few minutes late, hand-in-hand with "her girl." I have to admit I was less than thrilled—while it didn't matter to me if she was straight or lesbian, I did have hopes of becoming really good friends with Jo. Such is life. Jo was smiling and I knew she was happy which was all that mattered.

After the customary introductions, Jo and Heather explained that the reading wasn't taking place until about eight so we had plenty of time to burn. We decided to head over to Heather's place where I'd gathered Jo was staying lately. Once there we'd talk, have a drink or two and fix up something to eat.

As it turned out Heather's place was a beautiful loft on Commercial. It was decorated in a lot of Japanese-style gear and looked fantastic. Jo seemed in her element wandering around with calligraphy on the walls, bonsai scattered around the loft.

"This place is great," I said under my voice to Jo as Heather headed to the kitchen to make up a bunch of macaroni and cheese—the dinner of champions.

"Isn't it? When I saw her place for the first time I realized that this girl had some taste. But she's more into the look than the philosophy, which is just fine."

In no time we'd filled our insides and were gearing up to get going.

They really were a great couple. Even though I felt somewhat jilted I was happy to be with people so full of joy from simply being together—it was a good change from the way I'd gotten used to spending my evenings.

The bar was as cool as Jo had described. Named after some writer I'd never heard of that Jo was certain I "had to know," it was a throw back to a time when you'd find poets and so called "Beatniks" hanging out getting drunk, stoned or whatever with poetry and prose flooding the air.

The crowd inside was of the Commercial Street type—artistic, free-thinking and well dressed.

I have to admit I was more than a little surprised to hear that the writers we were coming to listen to were from the Sunshine Coast, the place I'd vanished from however long ago.

While I didn't know them I knew of them. Both were writers I'd wanted to read but never got around to. Frank Fowler was the original Beatnik of the duo, I can remember reading a story about him when I'd just moved to the Sunshine Coast about his days as a poet-logger. He was considered a grandpa of contemporary Canadian poetry—and he looked the part, dressed from head-to-toe in black, with a turtle-neck sweater curled around his gentle-looking pale face. On his head he wore the kind of hat you'd expect to see on a sea captain, fisherman—or an old logger. He looked a little nervous while glancing around at the crowd that was beginning to fill the room.

His cohort in crime I'd heard about from a friend before I took off. John Baker—the name even sounded like someone you'd expect to be a street writer. And that is exactly what he was. He was rugged, tough looking with silver hair combed back to the point of precision. When my friend told me about him I had to admit I thought he was pulling my leg. Baker was a former tough guy from Philadelphia who had somehow found his way to

Gibsons, writing books and making art but not before holding down just about every job you could imagine and having been an adventurer in South America where he found a lost city in the jungle.

As I looked at Baker who sat slyly in a shiny silver suit jacket drinking a beer like it was art, I could remember saying to my friend, "fuck off...why would he be living here?" when he'd first told me about him.

But it was all true and likely there was more that only Baker knew about. Looking at the two of them sitting there together having a great time I grinned remembering my friend's answer, "why wouldn't he be living here—you have to live somewhere."

He was right and these two were something else, just like everyone said. They may have been lost prophets in the wilderness but they were doing what they wanted, where they wanted.

We found a seat in the back and ordered a couple of beers and relaxed as some guy got up and introduced Fowler and Baker, thanked the owner of the bar for having them and then wandered off.

A jazz band started playing and Baker walked up to the mike. Before he even spoke you knew you were about to hear magic— and it was. With the band jamming behind him, he hoisted a book in the air, holding the mike stand with the other hand. Words rolled out like music, we all sat there waiting for every word to drop out of his mouth.

Jo leaned over and said something about Baker being the next best thing to Kerouac.

"This guy doesn't need to be compared to anyone—he's great."

The crowd went wild when he finished, slowly closing his book, grinning.

Soon Fowler was up. He held the mike stand like an old

whaler would stand on the deck of his ship with harpoon in hand. Like Baker before him, Fowler was something else. He read poems about the death of his father and mother, images of an empty swing that he'd once been pushed in seemed to fill the air around us. Jo wiped her eyes and looking around I noticed everyone else was caught up in Fowler's words too.

While the jazz seemed to send the words into the air, Fowler didn't need the push—he was hot steam, filling the air with his weavings of words.

After they were done Jo, Heather and I just sat there staring at them sitting drinking at their table.

"That was something."

"They are good, better than good. Listening to them read makes me remember why we're all here," I said.

Heather and Jo looked at me obviously expecting me to add something intelligent.

"I mean these are guys who have been to the bottom and have climbed out of it and not only learned enough to write about it but have the gift to be able to teach us all."

Jo nodded. "I thought you'd enjoy this. These guys write about real life—the street but it doesn't drag them down. I think you and I both could learn something special from them."

I looked back over at the two writers patting each other on the shoulder toasting a job well done with a pint each.

"I really need to get my shit together don't I," I said looking back at Jo.

"I don't know. But what I do know is that if you don't take life by the horns and live it'll take you. If you don't get yourself together one way or another the junk will kill you."

I could hear the two friends laughing, I wondered if they were happy to be finished or just happy to be together.

After we finished another set of drinks we wandered back to

Heather's place where we sat talking about the night, the great writing and other great writers, and about living life like an adventure.

Heather had to work the next day and excused herself, Jo again noted that I was welcome to crash on the couch. I nodded, agreeing that I didn't really have anywhere else to go.

I smiled but was really starting to feel like my body was slowly being jabbed with slivers of glass. The pain was growing.

"Thanks for a great night Jo. I just want you to know that whatever happens I'm just happy to have met you."

She rubbed my head and gave me a peck on the cheek. I felt safe.

"Anything you need you just ask. I know people who can help, all right—if I can do it so can you."

I settled down to sleep but was hurting too much for my eyes to close. In the darkness all I could think about was Ginger back at her apartment struggling to figure out a way to shoot up without doing it herself.

As quietly as I could I found a piece of paper and a pen and scribbled, "thank you, just couldn't sleep—too comfortable," and snuck out the door.

# Ginger

She was already long dead when I got there, letting myself in through the fire escape like I often had to when she was passed out.

At first I thought she was just sleeping but then I noticed she wasn't breathing.

I just sat there looking at her cold body on the floor. There was a needle only a few feet from her so I figured she'd finally given herself a fix but had totally fucked something up.

Grabbing the phone I started to dial 911 but only got as far as 9. My finger hovered above the keypad. I looked at Ginger and slowly put the phone down.

Almost like watching myself, my body stood, walked over to where Ginger kept her drugs and cash (under the bed), put it into my pockets and headed back out the window. I was halfway through when I realized what I was doing and turned back to look at the corpse sprawled on the floor of the rundown apartment. Slowly I reached into my pocket and pulled the heroin back out, looking at it for what felt like a long time.

I saw my hand reach out and drop the bag on the window sill. Standing on the fire escape I closed the window and headed back down into the cold dark alley and then into the streets.

# Wandering

The night dragged by slower than it ever felt like it had gone before. I spent most of it in pain. I wanted to go back and get stoned, dead body or not.

Finally, to stop myself from the temptation I called 911 and told them about Ginger.

I can't remember much more about the night except wandering around quiet streets moaning, my body shaking and tears raining endlessly down my cheeks.

I wanted to call Mary, my long dead mother, my father who was likely off somewhere with his most recent young girlfriend as out of touch as ever, or anyone for that matter—but instead I somehow forced myself to keep walking.

At some point in the night I managed to find my way back to Heather's place—how I don't know, but the fact that the next morning she was kneeling beside me while I shivered and shook in front of her apartment makes me pretty sure I got there somehow.

With muscle power alone she managed to haul me up and dragged me back into her place. As she helped me to the couch which was still made up with blankets I looked at her and for the first time in a very long time I felt a twinge of shame at how I must look.

"I need help..." I managed to say.

By this time Jo had come out of somewhere and was helping to take off my soaked clothes and put me on the couch.

I don't know if it was the withdrawal, or a nervous break-down but as I looked at my own body I couldn't help but feel sorry for myself. And even though I smelled awful from a night of pissing on myself in the street—and likely looked much worse—Jo put her arm around me, smoothed back my hair and said, "everything is going to be all right."

I tried to tell her about Ginger and about wanting to clean up but I'm not sure if I even understood what was coming out of my mouth.

All I remember before closing my eyes and passing out was her—though it sounded more like the voice of God—saying, "don't worry, you'll be all right—I'm going to help you."

# Quickening

The days that followed weren't the kind you write home about.

Jo's deal was pretty basic—I get the help she could give me as long as I stayed clean. It was a good deal but easier to agree to than to follow.

It was only in going cold turkey that I realized just how far I'd gone—how hooked I really was.

At some point I asked Jo what day it was but realized that I had no idea when it was that I first ran and started using. Everything was so cluttered. But it had been awhile, looking in the mirror for the first time in a long time I barely recognised the person looking back.

Cleaning up from drug addiction is no party. The hangover most people dread so much after a night of drinking pales in comparison to the torment of a junkie letting his skin heal.

Hell couldn't be much worse than heroin withdrawal.

I had seizures, hallucinations, and pain beyond imagination. And when I did sleep it was filled with terrifying visions of lost limbs and dead babies. In one ultra-vivid nightmare I watched myself take a chainsaw to Mary—worse yet, I couldn't shake myself awake.

Withdrawal is a torturous, dark, blood red hunger that reaches out to all facets of you. And the endless pain can only be described as exquisite. It might be an odd word to describe a thing you are sure at the time is going to kill you, but it is literally perfect in its torture, and extreme in its torment.

I remember reading somewhere that "what doesn't kill you makes you stronger." I didn't feel stronger. Tired, empty, pointless and stupid—but not stronger.

At the bad points during the withdrawal if someone had whispered in my ear that I'd feel much better if I cut off my head and swung it around by the hair—I'd have smiled and grabbed for a saw. Anything could have made sense in that world of fresh new pain and confusion.

But nonetheless, I made it through a few tough weeks.

When my teeth weren't chattering and my body shaking, Jo was keeping me busy teaching the finer points of her Buddhist philosophy—street Zen—she tutored me on meditation and the idea that by not trying, just flowing we can attain a simple peace.

"The truth to life is that death is always with us, looking over the shoulders of all of us. What we need to do as enlightened beings is to live in the now—just keep in mind that this may be your last moment of life, your last breath, your last conversation, your last chance at a good deed.  If you think this way you won't run from death but be thankful for it as being your greatest teacher and motivator."

A lot of what she said was very cool. The Bodhisattvas that she always talked about couldn't be any better than her. And after a couple weeks of her almost constant companionship I decided that if she wasn't a Bodhisattva there was no such thing.

When she wasn't busy teaching me she was throwing book after book at me, which I read like a man possessed. Books on the saints I always tried to talk about (but Jo was more interested in Buddhist conversation), books on nature, books on just about any topic you can imagine.

And so I was lead through hell by the hand of one of the most amazing people I'd ever met, someone I wanted badly to get closer to but someone just out of reach on more than one level.

As had to happen eventually, one morning I woke up, the sun was shining and birds were singing. I knew that things were different. I was a junkie on the other side of the junk. But still a junkie. Always a junkie.

# Eyes

The world had changed during those weeks that now seemed to have just flown by—but at the time felt like they'd never end.

The worst thing now was dealing with the lingering pain of guilt. Guilt that if I'd only done something different, maybe I could have saved Ginger from her lonely death in overdose.

But there was nothing I could do.

At some point I'd told Jo about Mary and what I'd done and as I was packing up to go—where to I wasn't quite sure—she asked me to call her, let Mary know I was all right. But it was a payment for services rendered that I just refused to pay.

Jo shook her head at me and asked where I thought I was going since I didn't have a home to go to.

"I don't know but I do know that Heather is starting to look at me like she wished I'd left a long time ago."

"You can't go back on the street, what if you get back into the same problem as before?"

I gave her a hug and told her I'd come back in a day or two, lying that I just needed to get out and stretch.

As soon as I stepped out the front door of the loft I realized everything was different. The world around me seemed bright and very loud.

Wandering around Hastings, past drug dealers and hookers

and assorted criminals and junkies I felt out of place where a month earlier I would have fit right in, joining them in conversations about nothing. But I was still out on the street, little different than anyone else and within a day I was back to getting meals with an outstretched hand or digging though a can of garbage looking for bottles. But everything was different, now I actually noticed what I was doing and felt somewhat remorseful and the worst part of all was that I saw the eyes watching me.

And increasingly the other street people scared me—a sea of grey, tattered rags, hair, dirt and putrid smells.

# Sanctuary

I wandered around for days, slowly becoming more and more lost in streets I was beginning to know better than my own hands and feet. The prostitutes and junkies were starting to look like family again and more than one dealer that approached me nearly pushed me over the edge into hell once again.

But instead I walked the streets all day long, deciding that while I had no place to go I could at least give myself and the rest of the world the illusion of movement. So I walked.

I'd walk all day, pausing only to look for bottles and cans in dumpsters and when darkness fell, I'd walk most of the night too. When fatigue pushed in on my spirit I'd sleep as far away as possible from those places I knew the junkies slept. Instead of sleeping in parks or in doorways, I'd climb fire escapes to sleep on the roof of buildings. And blanketed under a sea of stars I'd snooze as best I could. Truth was that I couldn't get more than a few hours of sleep every night—the fear of the street was becoming too real, and ever present.

And as fear tends to do, it led to stupid, reckless behaviour. I found myself creeping around the fire escapes or looking through the windows of nearby buildings, watching women sleep, people making love—just about anything I could see. It beat picking on my old scars that still lay under the sleeves of my shirt. Looking in on the lives of these people made me feel better, knowing that while life seemed detached and out of reach to me right now, there was hope for things to change.

It was during one of these nights, perched on some rooftop that I first saw the Buddhist temple.

Ancient looking and somehow completely out of place, even in this mismatched city. It was one of the most beautiful buildings I'd ever seen. Just the way it sat there in the darkness—or maybe it was just me putting something into it myself. Whatever it was, I knew that come morning I'd have to stick my nose in those doors and see what I could see.

Even with great plans for the next day and images of meeting enlightened old monks who'd teach me the secrets of the universe, sleep was still sleep on the roof of a building. And when I did drift off to dreams, they were filled of images of playing on the beach with a child whose face I couldn't quite make out. I'd look as close as I could but took frustration to new heights with my inability to see what I needed to see. Every time I'd move closer, this laughing creation of my mind would turn, or move just enough that I could never quite make out who it was. But there was something familiar in the laugh. Something haunting.

Morning, needless to say, came as a blessing.

Using some of the change I'd gathered up the day before from bottle returns I grabbed myself a warm coffee and some prepackaged processed something from a convenience store down the street from the temple. It was cheap and filled the gap in my gut and quieted down the growls.

It was still early morning when I saw people starting to file into the temple through a small graffiti-covered door. I ran across the street through an opening in the morning traffic, eyes fixed on that door—why would anyone spray graffiti on the door of a Buddhist temple? I noticed that under thin layers of paint on the wall facing the road you could still make out the tracings of yet more paint signatures.

Reaching for the door I took a breath of air feeling a bit uncertain about what I was doing but not letting myself chicken out of wandering in.

As the door opened I could instantly smell incense and was greeted by a large pile of shoes in front of a huge statue of Buddha.

"When in Rome, do as the Romans do," I thought to myself.

Wandering into the temple I felt like I'd entered another world. The incense mingled with chanting and the sound of bells and wooden blocks being struck together.

In a large room surrounded by massive golden figures of various Buddhist characters about 20 people sat unmoving. No one looked up at me, no one showed me where to sit or what to do, so I sat in the back—grinning from ear-to-ear but trying hard not to.

I don't know if it was the incense or the chanting or everything combined but I have no idea how long I sat there. It was as if time had checked itself at the door when I came in. And that was fine—strange—but fine.

I was not certain what was happening or what had happened only moments earlier, but people eventually started getting up and moving back to the pile of shoes, hanging up their long black robes and silently heading back out the door.

There were a few bows, a couple smiles but not one person said two words. There was someone tending to things around the temple—but it wasn't even a monk. Or at least not a monk like I'd imagined I would find.

With little other choice, except for perhaps sitting around talking to myself I decided to head out, happy I'd experienced something different but a little uncertain what exactly that something was.

Just as I was about to head out the door I saw a man in robes at one end of the temple. He was watching me.

Not quite sure what else to do I bowed to him. He smiled and bowed back.

"This is it, the moment I've been waiting for," I mumbled to myself and walked over to him, thinking how much I wished Jo was with me.

When I was only a few feet away he looked up from the work he was doing sorting through some books. He smiled.

"Hi there."

He was still smiling.

"I was just wondering if you were a monk?" I asked, feeling a little stupid as I stared at his bald head thinking to myself as I did, whether he was bald or just really well shaved—it seemed like his head was shining.

"M-monk?" he repeated.

"Are you a Buddhist monk?" I said motioning to the temple around us.

"Buddha?" he said raising his long haired eyebrows.

"I came here today to learn about Buddhism. But I didn't really understand anything that went on."

"On...Buddha..."

He was still smiling at me but I have to admit that the last thing I felt like doing was smiling. I don't think I could smile even if I wanted to, with every brain cell working hard to figure out how to communicate without language. Wishing I was telepathic.

"How long have you been in B.C.?"

Crumpling his brow he just looked at me.

"How long have you," I pointed at him, "been in B.C.?" I realized it was small talk but I figured if I could get to a common level we'd be making some progress.

"U. B. C.?"

Now I was confused.

"How long have you been in B.C.? How long have you been a monk here?" I scratched my head.

"U. B. C.?" He was smiling again.

I had no idea if he was talking about the University of British Columbia, asking me if this was B.C., if I was from B.C., or just clarifying my question.

Smiling to myself I realized that the only enlightenment I was going to be having in this temple today was simply that I needed get out of the fantasy world of meeting enlightened old monks who were going to teach me all the meanings to the universe. Or at least it wasn't going to happen here and on this day.

I bowed to him slowly and waved saying a simple, "thank you." He bowed back still smiling as I turned and walked away.

After throwing my shoes back on my feet I opened the doors to the temple and was welcomed back into the outside world with the roar of traffic. As the door closed I thought about how behind the closed door of the temple it was easy to forget the kind of world that spun around just on the other side of the walls.

Maybe that's why the graffiti was left on the door—a kind of reminder to those entering exactly what it was they were leaving behind.

# Flights

Wandering the streets after a morning of foreign religious exercise left me feeling a little blue—not about the religion, but about the fact that I'd had such lofty goals only a short time earlier and walked away a little more confused than when I walked in.

For one reason or another I decided to jump on the SkyTrain and just ride. For those who don't know about it, the SkyTrain is Vancouver's version of a subway—and it's the best. The train travels without a driver, mostly above ground and gives some of the best views of Vancouver that can be seen. It's cheap (if you pay) and is a great way to spend the day when you have little else to do.

I've always had a thing for trains and while the SkyTrain isn't a luxury trip across the Orient it's pretty much as close to the real thing as you get in Vancouver—and it's fun. The best seat on the train is up front where the driver would sit if the things weren't automated or at the very back of the last car. When I was a kid I used to sit up front with only the thin piece of glass separating me from the open air and the track below. I learned a long time ago that if you scootch up really close to the glass and forget about the people sitting behind you, and just stare straight forward it can feel like you're flying along those tracks.

So after sneaking into the cars—there are rarely train cops

watching for people snagging free rides—I had grand plans of sitting in that front seat for the rest of the day. Or at least until I got caught, hungry, bored or a multiple of other scenarios. Unfortunately someone else had the same idea.

At first I thought the kid with the backpack was just going to sit staring out of the front of the train for a few stops and then get off but when stop after stop went by I realized I wasn't going to get my choice seat. Worst of all, after about four stops he turned and started poking through his bag, not even using the window.

I guess he caught wind of the fact I was staring at him because he started sneaking looks back my direction like you learn in highschool—like looking out the window just behind me and other covert ways.

But instead of playing along I decided that friendliness was probably the best option. "Hey..."

He nodded at me with a little surprised look on his face.

"Nice day for a ride on the SkyTrain, eh?" I said smiling, trying to be as friendly as possible, half hoping that he'd decide I was some sort of slobbering loonie and move to the back of the car.

"Sure is...I love riding this thing. I like to ride it because of the calm it gives me."

"Oh yeah? That's wild...I'm kind of doing the same thing. Feeling a little frazzled and worn out, thought about all the fun I used to have riding this thing when I was a kid."

He started fumbling through his bag again.

"You lost something?"

"No. I jumped on the SkyTrain hoping to get some ideas for a paper I'm writing for school."

"What you writing about?" I asked sliding over to a seat a little more convenient for conversation.

"I'm studying theology and I decided to write a paper about saints and rapture."

I sat looking a little blankly at the student.

"Sorry...about levitation and the religious relevance of it."

I couldn't believe my ears. "You mean St. Joseph of Copertino...he's the greatest of all of the flying saints."

"Actually there were a lot of them—from around the world too, not just those in the Catholic church. There have been Hindu, Tibetan Buddhist, and various others. The thing that I find so interesting is the way these people—all really religious— are treated by their fellow holy people."

I just looked at this young man waiting for more.

"Take St. John of the Cross...and others...they were turned over to the Inquisition by those in and around them, censured and condemned, held as prisoners and threatened with excommunication or death, all for the crime of having a religious experience unlike anything the rest of us can understand."

Nodding slowly I could feel the grin on my face getting bigger as I realized that while I had expected to have some sort of deep experience at the temple it took jumping the SkyTrain to get me there.

"So you think they levitated because of a religious experience?"

He looked at me nodding. "I think there is some sort of religious element to the levitation process but I think there is something more too. In almost all of the cases of levitation it appears to be a simple, almost effortless event when the individual is completely in the moment—a kind of blast of enlightenment that actually makes you lighter. But I'm not sure at all, I've never experienced it and haven't met anyone who has done it themselves. It just amazes me that the people you'd think would welcome such events tend to treat those who can do it as threats."

"Why do you think that is?" I asked.

"I'm not sure." He looked out the window at the buildings

passing by. "Maybe it has something to do...at least in the Catholic case that the church didn't want to lose its grip on the idea that the population had to go through them to get to God. They had and have a very strict way of things with the Pope at the top. If a simple and sometimes not-too-bright monk can fly in a moment of rapture, like St. Joseph did, seeming to be more in touch with God than the Pope was, it could be seen as a bad thing. A loss of control."

"Do you think anyone can levitate or is it something that only some people can do for whatever reason?"

He shrugged his shoulders pulling a bunch of books out of his bag. "I've been reading all of these books looking for just that answer. There is documentation of monks in Tibet who were seen levitating and other stories of yogis. It doesn't seem to be a Catholic-only thing. I think that the mind needs to be in a certain still state. A place where the self is no longer in control, where the laws or those laws that we have talked ourselves into believing control our lives no longer apply. A self-less state where the 'you' that you really are can do some amazing things."

"I've heard of other holy people who can make things appear and others who can set fire with their minds alone."

"I think that idea of the holy man, someone who has set himself...or herself, apart from the rest of us is one part of the key. These are people who are dedicated to finding the truth, willing to do whatever it takes and often throwing themselves into the wild of the mind or the wild of reality to do it."

"You learned all this from those books?"

He looked down a little embarrassed at saying so much to a complete stranger. But I was enthralled at the words coming from this young student. So much insight for someone so young.

"I've thought about this stuff quite a bit—the books just help the thoughts to come and give a reference point to start from. But I don't really think you can learn from books, you learn from experience—books are just kind of like turning on a light but it's up to you to poke around the room and see what is in there, books just help you to see."

We both grinned at each other. One of those perfect moments in time where we were both in the right place, talking to the right person at the exact moment we needed it.

"Do you think that these people are different from the rest of us?"

He leafed through the pages of one of his books as if the answer would just leap out and grab hold of him.

"I think it's like I said, they are just open to the potential of the moment and somehow pull the cork out of the bottle of human potential."

"Do you think you or I would ever be able to do something like that?" I asked hoping to get an answer that would make a life-time of dreaming come closer to reality. But instead he just sat there smiling.

"What?"

"Nothing," he said cracking his smile for only a second.

"So...what do you think—it has always been a kind of dream of mine to do what St. Joseph did...I mean apart from the Inquisition...the thought of being able to levitate, backwards or not."

"St. Joseph was a very holy man. He was dedicated to his faith—even when other religious men of the time had less perfect faith and ridiculed him, St. Joseph never wavered. Do you think you could handle that?"

I looked at him wondering where he'd come from. How it was possible for someone to be sitting exactly where I had planned on sitting and know so much about the very things I'd been thinking about?

"I've always aspired to be a man on some sort of holy path. I guess I'm just having trouble finding the on-ramp that leads to that way."

"You should read everything you can on the subjects. And just look in those right directions and towards the right people. If you're supposed to find something you'll find it."

The automated voice announced that the car was about to stop. As we slowed I looked at this student and his pile of books.

"You're probably right. But you know what you can do right now?"

"What?"

He looked nervous.

"Put those books in the bag and hand them over."

The car was coming to a stop.

"Put the fucking books in the bag and give them to me. Don't cause a scene...just hand them over." I couldn't believe what my voice was saying.

At first I didn't think he was going to do what I'd asked him to and was somewhat afraid of what I'd do next—and more than a little uncertain of what exactly I should do.

But thankfully it didn't come to that.

We sat there for what felt like an eternity like two gun-slingers waiting for the first opening to draw and shoot.

Without moving his eyes from me, the student quickly stuffed his books back into the bag and threw it at me.

"Just take them and leave then. I just hope that one day you'll be ashamed at yourself for what you've done."

Getting up and shouldering his backpack while jumping for the door which was already starting to close I shouted, "fuck you. The one thing life has taught me so far is that if I want to get anywhere I'm going to have to do it myself."

"St. Joseph would have been really proud of you."

The door closed and the car quickly sped off.

# Books

I stood there for a few minutes watching as the train travelled down the track, feeling both sick and a strange sense of excitement at the same time.

"I just stole a bag of books from a student for no reason other than the fact that I wanted them," I said to myself.

I knew there was more to it. I felt some sort of resentment at the fact this young kid knew more about the saints that I'd aspired to be like for most of my life. And of course there was the fact that I wanted his books.

It's amazing the kind of crap that will rip through your mind when you're fighting your ethics. Nodding to myself I gave some inner assurance that not only was I destined to meet him on the SkyTrain and get his bag, but that it was not really much different than panhandling or digging through garbage cans for bottles. In one book Jo had given me to read on the Bushido, the warrior path of the Japanese samurai, it talked about how even in battle, killing an opponent can be used as a method leading to enlightenment as long as the action is done in a state of pure-minded nowness. I was certain that my action was a no-minded, instant action that all the old Zen stories wrote about—crazy wisdom.

Of course someone else would have said my action was callous and without thought—somewhat different than a pure Zen-like act. But I put that out of my mind—or tried to.

The SkyTrain was out of sight now.

Pulling the bag higher on my shoulder I headed for the stairwell down to the street. I knew full well that if this kid was any bit as bright as he appeared to be he would have notified the police as soon as possible, so sticking around the area would be a bad mistake on my part—luckily the train hadn't taken me too far from downtown and after walking down a few alleys I was sure that I could make it back to my more regular haunts with little trouble.

Not really wanting to sit on a street corner reading books on religion I decided to head for the rooftop I slept on the night before.

Walking, thinking about what I'd done, the conversation on the train kept coming back into my mind. I tried to think about the books in the bag and the Buddhist temple earlier in the day but none of it was working. My own brain wasn't a good companion on the long walk back.

By the time I'd reached the building and crawled up the fire escape from the back alley careful to not draw any attention, which meant avoiding anyone who could see me, it was nearing suppertime. But thankfully it was still bright enough outside to read, so I sat there devouring the pages of the stolen books.

For at least a couple hours I sat digging through the pages. This student knew what he was doing—they were great. Some old, some new but all of them were just jammed full of amazing information.

I learned about the lesser details of the lives of this saint and how some other saint was ridiculed. But mostly I learned just what the student had said—these individuals were mostly like anyone else, except for the fact they had a tremendous level of faith. Even when they were being persecuted they kept to the simple fact that they were holy people intimate with something greater than themselves.

Reading about them and their arrests for performing miracles made me feel far less than proud about the fact I'd stolen books from a theology student and was reading them in hiding on the roof of a building doubling as my bedroom.

I put the books back into the bag, noticing that one of the outside pockets had something in it. Opening it up I found a wallet. No money but plenty of identification.

Pulling out an ID card with a picture and the name Mel Schutz under it, I sat there looking at the young face of the friendly kid I'd ripped off. Looking at the card it seemed as if good old Mel was looking back at me, staring me down once again as if in wonder of how I could have ever stolen his books.

Hauling myself up I made sure the bag was all closed up and headed back down to the street. If I was going to get any sort of insight it wasn't going to be through someone else's misery. That paper Mel said he was writing wasn't getting closer to being finished with the books he needed on a rooftop with me.

It was getting late but I was going to hike around the city all night if it took that long—I needed to find a cop, I needed to turn in the bag so that Mel could get that paper done that he was supposed to be writing.

After wandering around the streets for a couple of hours I learned first hand the simple truth that it is always hardest to find a police officer when you need one.

I was just about to give up and throw the bag into a mail box and hope for the best when (as happens when you decide to do something) I eventually found a cop tending to a small altercation between two bums on East Hastings.

Not wanting to give too much information or answer any questions I threw it on the hood of his car and yelled over to him that it was, "some student's books...found them. There is identification in the outside pocket."

He nodded an understanding of what I was saying and went right back to the intense conversation that he was trying to calm down, stuck between the drunk breath of the two men.

Seeing this young cop doing his best to stop the drink-blind men from hurting each other (and themselves) I smiled. There are moments in time when you can see exactly what turns the gears of an individual. In the eyes of that young cop I could see nothing except compassion and understanding. It was a great thing to witness and made me feel even more guilty, which at the moment felt just about right.

As I wandered down the street, the slurred yells echoing off the buildings and reverberating towards me, I decided right there and then that while I'd gotten my life back together getting off the drugs and getting off the street somewhat, I still had a long way to go to reach that kind enlightened bliss that Jo had pointed me towards. Not only that but I was still on the run and now dropped to the low of stealing books from students—not exactly a hardcore criminal but one more step down this path and I'd end up arrested and answering questions and explaining things about who I was and where I'd been that I didn't even want to think about. Not only that, but the fact that I could stoop so low without much thought scared the shit out of me, if I could steal books from a friendly stranger on the SkyTrain how hard would it be to continue fighting the urge to beat the boredom, release myself from my day to day torment with another fix?

Things had to change, I knew it. But even worse was the fact that I couldn't get Mel's last words out of my head as I jumped through the doors of the SkyTrain, shouldering his bag, "... St. Joseph would have been really proud of you."

# Boots

For whatever reason I decided that night that I wasn't going to sleep on a rooftop—climbing up to the top and looking back down at the world was a kind of gift for myself for a job well done. But after the majority of my day spent running from memories of my dumb crime I decided a secluded doorway in an alley was what I deserved.

It was a chilly night, taking me back to times when my addiction would have drowned out at least some of the sensation of sleeping in a doorway in a putrid smelling alley. But now I was clean and sleeping in a doorway was exactly that. No matter how much I tried I couldn't get comfortable, the smell of piss was overpowering and the sound of rats was deafening. And then there were the mumblings from a couple of older gentlemen in the adjoining large boxes assembled beside a dumpster.

I think I must have finally been drifting off after literally hours of twisting and turning, trying to find some way to get a balance of the torments to the point where all of them were at least bearable—and then I was jolted awake.

There wasn't a scream or a sound you'd expect in a dark alleyway, only laughter.

At first I thought it was just a bunch of people passing through on their way to some place better, and then I heard, "hey, there's another one over here..."

I opened my eyes quick enough to start moving away from the first set of boots that were flying at me on the ends of legs belonging to someone, who in my half asleep daze, I'd thought was Jo but very soon realized belonged to a group of big boot-wearing skinheads.

Between covering myself best I could to avoid the kicks, I could see that the two older bums were getting it pretty bad by the gang. The skinheads, dressed in bomber jackets, suspenders dangling nearly to their knees, and boots—normal enough looking footwear but more than savage as they tore into flesh.

I could see the face of one of the old men, broken toothed, hands quivering to cover his face as they continued to kick into him.

There is a hell reserved for watching another tortured in front of you, unable to do anything except continue to witness the horror.

"You people are worthless shit, an embarrassment to our race," a voice yelled down at me. I couldn't know if it was coming from the guy kicking me, from God or from someone watching from above. But between kicks I figured it must be coming from my attacker.

Lucky for me, being in the doorway afforded at least some protection against the attack as I squeezed my body closer into the corner, covering my head, curling into a ball.

"Shit, it's the police..." a voice yelled and the kicking stopped. I started praying that if the beating continued I'd get knocked unconscious. But it didn't. The skinhead grabbed my hair, pulling me face to face with him. I could smell the peppermint gum he had in his mouth. "You didn't see anything here you fucking piece of shit. We'll kill you next time..." He let go and then they were gone.

I could hear them running down the damp pavement still

laughing as they went. But even still, I didn't rush to get up, shaking, curled in a fetal position waiting for another attack.

Eventually I decided it would be best for me to get up. I was somewhat confused about what had happened, still feeling half asleep. But my body screamed in a pain that I'd never really felt in my life before. I was sure that if my ribs weren't broken they were bruised pretty good.

There were no police in sight, so either they'd caught sight of the gang of skins and taken hunt, or the shaven headed thugs were just out to lunch. Whatever the answer, the result was still the same—I needed to get out of the alley before they decided to come back and finish what they'd started.

I looked over to the old men writhing on their cardboard beds. "Are you guys going to be all right?"

No answer.

I could hear them whimpering just a few feet away but couldn't see anything, just some movement under cardboard.

Getting up I pulled myself over to the old guys' pile of trampled home and started lifting the large pieces out of the way.

"Just get the fuck out of here you motherfuckers," one of them screamed at me covering his face.

At first I thought I should explain that I'd just been beaten as well but thought it would be for best if I just left them alone. I had to take care of myself. "Do you want me to call for an ambulance?"

"Just get the fuck out of here. Don't fuck around with us or we'll fuck you right up," one of them said trying to hoist himself up, either punch drunk or completely wasted.

"Hey man I just got the shit kicked out of me too. I just want to help...make sure you're all right..."

He looked down at his pal who was moaning and bleeding and then back up at me, blood running down his face from a gash on his forehead and what looked like a broken nose. "You fuck-ers tried to kill us! What did we ever do to you? Heh? What did we do to deserve this?"

Crying, he turned his attention to his friend.

I realized that nothing I could say was going to help so instead decided I'd better just leave them alone like they wanted.

Cradling my ribs I turned and headed for the street where it was at least well lit and would lead somewhere better than a piss drenched alley that you couldn't even get a minute's worth of sleep in.

# Road

After a couple days of wandering around, trying my best to stay away from pretty much everyone, including Heather's loft or Jo's newspaper office (although both were the only places I knew I'd feel safe) and paranoid of the police finding me in connection with the "great theology book heist," the skinheads bumping into me, or some other street person or junkie talking to me, I decided with a calm certainty that I either had to get out of the city or jump off the nearest bridge.

Even though I spent a lot of time trying to stop myself from going to her, feeling like a failure once again, Jo was the first person I tracked down—who else was I going to tell I wanted to get out of this concrete prison?

"Great, does this mean you're going back home to your wife?" she asked with that innocent but all-knowing face.

"Not exactly. What I think I'm going to do is hit the road. You know—like those writers we saw on that first night—I want to meet life head-on instead of hiding from it here."

She smiled.

I couldn't help but begin to feel a little tight in the pants. She really was beautiful—her shaved head only accenting her beauty (much different than the same hair style I'd seen on the gang a few nights previous and with much different results).

I'm sure she knew quite well that I wanted her but I was fully aware of the situation. Not to mention the fact she probably saw me as some dead-beat who didn't have the courage to let his family know he was alive.

# Highways

Being the Bodhisattva she was, Jo took me to the bus station and even gave me a big chunk of cash, more than enough for a ticket, some grub and future expenses. She was great—either that or she was just glad to get me out of her hair—so to speak.

It didn't really matter. With a peck on the cheek and a grinning wave I was gone.

I was headed north with no real plan.

I gazed out the window at the grey blur going by—watching all the people and buildings, the alleys and streets.

It was good to be leaving Vancouver for the open air country that is the majority of British Columbia. The same rugged world that had basically stayed unchanged for the past one hundred years except for in small communities here and there. And in no time at all, I was nearly there.

The mountains of concrete and glass became smaller and smaller, making way for other mountains—these much more impressive.

I grinned, running my hands down my legs almost making sure that I was really doing what I was doing.

Pulling my coat (which Jo had washed herself and smelled great) around me and smiling at my familiar reflection in the window I hunched down in the seat, closed my eyes and looked into the future.

# Signposts

B y the time the bus pulled into Kamloops I was already quite certain I'd had enough of bus travel. Or if not enough of the bus, I'd had my fill of the kids screaming and kicking the seat behind me.

I tried to use some of that Zen-like patience that Jo had tried her hardest to sink into me and I thought I'd have in abundance but only ended up catching myself shooting them looks of death every time they peered around the seat at me.

As I stood on the sidewalk watching the bus roll away without me I had a strange feeling—even though I was glad to be rid of it, I felt very alone, for the first time in a long time. And strange enough it felt nice.

At first I thought I might hang out in Kamloops for a little while but after wolfing down some eats while watching traffic fly by outside I decided even Kamloops was too much of a city for me at this point in time.

In the parking lot I walked up to a group of truckers with the hope of snagging a ride north. Well, the gods that look after broke ex-junkies bumming their way across B.C. on the run from something must have been smiling at me. The first trucker I gabbed at said he was bobtailing his tractor to Salmon Arm and was turning around and heading up to Prince George a few days after that.

While I wasn't born there, I'd spent most of my life in

Salmon Arm and (as happens) was thrilled to leave when Mary and I decided we were headed for the Sunshine Coast—but by the day after our move I was already feeling like I was missing a part of me.

"I'd love to head to Salmon Arm," I grinned at this first class Bodhisattva—my second in such a short time—by the name of Ben. He was big, round and when he smiled you couldn't help but wonder if he could see through his smile-squinted eyes.

I told him he reminded me of Hotei—the big bellied Buddha Jo called her favourite. I was already starting to miss her.

"Is that his name...Hoo-tea..." Ben said looking out at the road.

"Hotei actually," I smiled back.

"Why do you figure he's always smilin'—or did he just have something good to eat or maybe in on some Buddha joke."

I watched as Ben drove, changing gears without even thinking. "I think he's probably smiling because he's free from all the ties that bind I guess. He doesn't have anyone to worry about and doesn't allow himself to become deluded or distracted from the way."

"What way?"

"The way—the road he is travelling. Did you know that Hotei carried around a big sack full of toys and candy? He'd just travel around laughing—pure Buddhism, giving joy to little kids, then he'd be back on his way."

"That's kind of cool. Guess he was some kind of Buddha Santa," Ben's face puckered up, giggling to himself, his whole body rolling along.

"I don't know if he was a Santa Buddha but he was a truck-er Buddha, travelling from town to town, up and down dirty and forgotten roads for the sake of all beings." I looked out the window realizing just how much Jo had rubbed off on me.

"I like that," Ben said. "So how do you know all of this—you some kind of Krishna or somethin'?"

I laughed thinking back on everything that had gone on in the past couple of months. "No, I guess I'm as far from anything to do with Buddhas as you can get—to be honest I don't really know what or who I am, that's the problem. But lately I think a lot about all this kind of stuff."

"Why do you say you don't know who you are and yet you seem to have a pretty good idea of what is going on."

"Those are just stories," I said realizing I was lying to him and myself by saying that. "There was a long while that I did everything I could not to think. But things are different now. I realized that closing my eyes didn't make things go away. So now, now I roll with the punches and get out and live to my fullest—or as good old Hotei would say, I'm putting the pack on my back and flowing."

Ben grinned, nodded and reached down to put a cool jazz tape in the stereo. "Is that what he'd say?"

We drove down the highway with the music blending with the trees and an occasional eagle circling in the air outside the cab.

# Visits

B en was even more the Bodhisattva/Saint than I thought he was.

Pulling into Salmon Arm for the first time since I left was strange—I just kept looking back and forth at all the changes. Without saying a word about dropping me off (or asking if there was anywhere I'd like to be dropped off) he pulled up in front of a bed and breakfast owned by one of his former trucker buddies. He headed in while I stayed in the truck. After a few minutes he came out to give me the deal (I'd have a place to stay as long as I helped out around the place) and then Ben would be back in a couple of days. That is, he'd be stopping early in the morning to pick me up if I still wanted a lift north.

"I'll be here Ben—and thanks."

He just squint-smiled and pulled the huge truck back onto the road.

Before heading in to find my room I spun my head around in a 360 degree circle (well almost) sucking in my former stomping ground. It was a great feeling to be back on familiar, friendly turf.

My years in Salmon Arm weren't the most exciting—especially looking back over the more recent past—but they felt safe. Moving away from that secure feeling was one of the hardest things I've ever done and one which always made me wonder if I'd made a mistake doing it.

Images of old-timers popped into my head, the same guys and gals that had lived in the town from their first breath and wouldn't leave until their last. I knew that I wasn't destined to be one of those people but couldn't help but wonder what it would be like to really call a town your own, knowing each and every crack in the pavement—a walking museum.

After organising things at the bed and breakfast I decided to hike downtown and see what there was to see—or at least what had changed since I'd left.

With Mt. Ida looming above, silently greeting me I couldn't help but marvel at how when I'd lived here all I wanted to do was leave and now that I was back I couldn't imagine why I'd ever wanted to go.

An isolated valley town on the Trans Canada Highway, Salmon Arm is a tight community on an amazing lake. It is a place that you really have to stay in to appreciate.

Midway on my trek downtown a van pulled over—I smiled knowing full well who it was and what I was in for.

Calvin McKenzie. His big freckled face grinned out from the driver seat. "Hey buddy—what you doing here? I thought you were dead."

I laughed. "If I am I'm one helluva hungry ghost."

"No really—everyone told me you were missing. Everyone guessed you'd either run off with a girl or were shark food."

I could see that even with his broad grin he was trying to be serious. I wandered closer to his open window. "I'm alive and well and came to town to see if you guys are keeping it in one piece—maybe have some fun. What are you up to?"

Calvin and I'd known each other since we were teens. If anyone was into having fun I knew it was him—I also knew that when he was having fun he'd be too busy to ask questions I didn't want to answer.

"Looks like I'm just done work and about to get shit-faced with you," he chuckled.

We both just stood our ground for a few minutes just glad to be seeing each other, smiling from ear to ear.

I tumbled into the van loaded with gear from work (telephone repair guy), grabbed Calvin's arm— "you don't know how great it is to see you." And it really was.

"Yeah, let's go drink."

At least some things never change.

As we pulled away and headed towards Calvin's place I looked down at the lake and the town wrapped around it—it felt like I'd never left. I half expected to see Mary wandering around the shops downtown.

But things had changed.

Calvin lived just a short hop from where he picked me up— actually everyone in Salmon Arm lives only a short hop from any other point in the town.

As we pulled into his driveway and made a bee-line for his basement I couldn't help but stare at the black toothpick-covered mountain that now made up a good chunk of Mt. Ida after fire burned it the summer after I left. It looked odd but even as crispy brown and black as she was, there was something impressive and beautiful about her.

I remembered hearing stories from native elders I'd met in out of the way places when I lived under the mountain's shadow, telling stories of the sacredness of the big old rock. One story that I've never been able to get out of my head concerns mythical "little people" they believed lived there—the same creatures that rescued their people in a time of famine. They were great stories— all pointing to the simple truth that the mountain endures. Long after famine, fires and little people are gone the mountain will remain towering above us all.

"You coming? Or do you plan on standing there looking at that burned up old mountain?" Calvin said taking off his boots in the doorway.

"I'm coming," I said wandering in behind him and kicking off my own boots.

From the door I could see Calvin's pride and joy—his basement bar.

It's a certain kind of guy that owns his own bar—especially when that bar is in the basement of his home. For Calvin, his bar was sacred. And to be honest, his bar in his lonely old basement could compete against most commercial pubs and win hands down.

Looking around you couldn't help but wonder how much money he made installing telephones.

Nonetheless, Calvin was a special kind of cat—19 forever. I admired his energy, and his stamina.

# Moving

Everything that followed arrival at Calvin's is a bit of a blur. I can remember laughing a lot. I can remember some girls I didn't know coming by and drinking with us, a little flirting—what happened next I couldn't tell you.

What I do know is that I woke up after about 10 hours or more of solid drinking with a head about the size of Idaho.

To say I wasn't feeling well is an understatement. I was still drunk and very hungover at the same time—the kind of drunk/hungover combination that you curse hiccups because of the fear of what they may be bringing.

Calvin hadn't changed a bit since I saw him last—he either had superior willpower, wasn't human or was just some kind of drinking machine.

While I prayed to the porcelain god Calvin made far too much noise in the kitchen, happily making breakfast—he even whistled while he did it, damn him.

"Hey Buddy—if you wanna party you gotta pay," he laughed through the door of the bathroom. I hurled the toilet scrub brush at the door. Calvin giggled again and made his way back to the kitchen where he continued to whistle and clang pots and make awful smells that made me feel even worse.

I did my best to be fun and interesting but finally the hangover got the best of me and without a goodbye or thanks—I grabbed my gear and hit the street.

The cold crisp air did me well as I trudged along the sidewalk.

I walked at a good clip, half fearing that Calvin would come after me. But I also knew he lived in his own world enough that he'd turn the channel on the television and forget that I was ever there.

So what now? I was too ill to eat, so heading to one of Salmon Arm's handful of restaurants was out of the question (strange fact that there are more churches in the Gem of the Shuswap than joints to grab a meal).

The other thing I decided as I stumbled back to the bed and breakfast was that I didn't want to meet any other old friends. I felt anti-social like you could only understand after the world's worst hangover.

So instead I settled for wandering around with a brain still swimming in the waters between realities.

Shoving my hands into the pockets of my coat I felt a piece of paper I didn't quite remember. I pulled it out and unfolded it, looking face to face with a picture of myself on a "missing" poster.

I could slightly remember Calvin throwing it at me sometime in the night while some female jabbed at me, breathing her booze breath on my skin.

Teetering on the sidewalk I tried to focus on what the page said, images of the past flowing by. I crumpled it into a ball and threw it over my shoulder, "fuck it."

The sun was still trying to poke it's head into the valley as I made my way back to the bed and breakfast and my warm room with it's puffy pillowed bed.

# Looking

By the time I finally pulled myself together and out of bed the sun was already going down.

"That is one day that is gone forever and I won't be able to remember," I mumbled to myself as I hoisted myself up in bed cracking my back and stretching.

Instead of hunting down another friend and catching myself another hangover I decided to stay put—especially after seeing the "missing" poster Calvin had given me. It was a great night so I decided to head outside and watch the night slowly blanket the mountains.

I grabbed a blanket, wrapped it over my shoulders, made myself a warm Earl Grey tea and headed out.

With no major city around Salmon Arm, watching the stars at night can really be something else—almost spiritual (it's just the mosquitoes that usually stop you from seeing God).

When I lived there and people came from out-of-town for a visit they'd often stand outside, jaws dropped, heads back, eyes to the skies.

You could see millions of stars, clusters of stars, shooting stars—it was an amazing experience.

Seeing space from that kind of perspective can really hit you with a whammy, making the viewer feel pretty insignificant.

The sky above us is so vast—each of those countless all seeing sparks with, perhaps, worlds of their own. It's hard not to wonder if somewhere out there, a person could be looking up at a very different looking sky, from a small town they feel so important in, looking back at you across time and space.

I spent hours like that. Sometimes sitting, sometimes standing but mostly reclined on the ground, arms behind my head just watching the heavens.

I mused to myself how life would likely be so much better if more people would take the time to grab a blanket and a warm tea, sit outside and just meditate under the stars. After all, what is more real, more important to our lives—our place in the universal grand scheme of things or that job, or paying those bills, or that television show?

I thought these thoughts and many others snugly under my blanket while the world around me whirled by—people huddled around their talking boxes or on their way to something they felt very important.

And even though I'm sure they'd argue that what the were doing was living, at that moment, looking skyward, wondering great wonderings, I knew much different.

# Chop wood, carry water

Mona, the woman of the place I was staying at, put me to work shortly after breakfast.

She smiled and said she had a little bit for me to do. Of course, this "little bit" took all day—but I didn't mind.

As I worked away I could remember Jo telling me of her time spent at a Zen temple down in Oregon. She was there for only a few weeks but a few things made a big impact on her—and on me after her telling. The most simple and profound lesson she learned there was the Zen training that could be found in the most mundane work, she called it, "the Zen-simple joys of work—good old fashioned chop wood, carry water, dig hole work."

She told stories of straight-backed smiling monks explaining that in Zen, all things can be an extension of meditation. And that walking, moving and working can all lead the person with the right mind to enlightenment.

So, with Jo's teaching rattling around in my brain I spent most of the day busy. I chopped wood, stacked it, cut down weeds, painted a door—all while trying to cultivate Buddhist mindfulness (as Jo had called it).

I can't say I came any closer to grasping any lost truths or glimpsed enlightenment but I did feel great and when I was done my mind felt clean and my body strong.

It was hard to think that only a few days earlier I had the great fortune of being woken from a miserable sleep by a gang of Aryan-something skinheads trying their best to kill me and those two helpless drunks. And hours before that I'd stolen a bag of books from a helpless student, and before that...

I knew that if Jo was with me she would have said something about living in the present.

Standing, sweat rolling down the small of my back I looked east towards far-off mountains and decided right there, with a sudden clarity like a hand smacking me upside the head, that I'd continue on my trek to wherever it was I was going.

I've always thought that everything in life happens for a reason. And so far things seemed to be pointing me towards some distant spot on that faraway horizon—a spot I had to get closer to.

# Night terror

When I hit the bed all the work from the day let loose in an orgasm of fatigue—I was sound asleep before my eyes closed. I jolted awake six hours later from such a deep sleep that I couldn't remember where I was for what seemed like an hour. I just sat there in bed sweating. I could faintly remember a terrible lingering nightmare that Mary had died in a car accident while looking for me.

Although so much time had gone by since I first took off, the dream seemed so real. And in my tired, half-waking confusion I thought it must be true—why else was the bed empty except for me? I looked around not quite sure where I was.

I reached for the phone realizing I wasn't in my home—but as the dial tone screamed out I realized I couldn't remember my phone number.

Reality started filtering its way back into my mind. I slowly remembered my run to the ferry, Mojo, shooting up, begging for money, Ginger dead, Jo helping me out and finally my escape from the city.

Then with the sound of the telephone wailing in the darkness I started crying, realizing everything I'd done.

I could feel the loss, the worry, and the confusion she must have felt when I disappeared. I thought about all the things I'd missed since my disappearance.

Putting the phone down and leaning back into my pillow I just lay in the dark, listening to the sound of the wind in the trees outside, staring at the red digital numbers on the alarm clock for what seemed like an eternity.

If there is a hell, I'm sure that it has nothing to do with fire and brimstone. Hell, if it exists, is full of loneliness and regret— tortured souls spending eternity wishing they'd done things differently or wondering why...and what if?

# Head start

Call it guilt or a bad night's sleep, but before the sun was even up I'd already grabbed my stuff, left a thank-you note and hit the road.

When I wandered out to the Trans Canada Highway I stood there for about five minutes, looking one way and then the other. One way leading back to the way I'd come and the other on towards the east.

Deciding the past was already behind me I turned my back once again to the west, pulled my jacket tight around me and trudged on with transport trucks rumbling past, throwing grit into my teeth.

After about an hour's walking and getting just barely out of Salmon Arm I decided I needed to hitch a ride—walking was getting me no where fast—so shouldering my small pack I stuck out my thumb.

I've never been the hitchhiking type but it was starting to really grow on me. Especially when after about an hour of trying I was picked up by a beautiful woman in a sports car.

I have to admit that at first I literally had to blink my eyes— I would have more expected to be picked up by some axe-weilding lunatic or escaped prisoner. But instead I looked into the red car and nearly tripped over my jaw when I saw the full package smiling back.

Blond hair, short skirt and a beautiful mouth—I couldn't have dreamed a better fantasy.

"Where are you going?" she asked stretching over to the passenger window where I was looking in. When she leaned over the plunging neckline on her red dress fell, exposing a glimpse of breasts bound in a lacy black bra that made me decide the rest of her was built just right too.

"I'm just headed east."

"So am I, hop in if you're interested."

I smiled and opened the car door. The leather seat made uncomfortable noises when I sat.

"Thanks a lot for the ride," I said putting on the seat belt and trying to be not too obviously checking her out as I looked around the car. "This is a great car you have here."

"Thanks. It belonged to my ex but now it's all mine."

The way she put the car into gear made me instantly jealous.

It turned out that she was just getting lost for the weekend, away from everything after a bad divorce. But she was the first to admit she got the better end of the settlement and planned on having some fun with her "earnings" as she called them.

She was really fun to drive with, she joked around, looked great and flirted up a storm. But the best part of all was the joy she took in stopping to read every single plaque she could find along the highway. We stopped at least twice every half hour—but with her for company I didn't mind at all. She treated me like we'd been friends for years.

By the time we finally made it to Revelstoke it was already afternoon, and Julie (as she told me her name was) decided we should stop for "drinks and a bite" at a hotel bar. She was the kind of woman you don't say no to, and besides, she was beautiful, and was giving me a free ride. Who was I to complain?

One drink quickly became two, three, four—I don't think

we ever did eat.

Before I knew it, Julie had her hands rubbing up and down my legs, unbuttoning my shirt and sneaking her fingers under the cloth feeling my chest.

Even though the room was slowly spinning, my anatomy was still functioning properly. And with the booze taking its toll on my control, it took me quite a bit to stop from jumping on her right there.

"What do you say we get a room tiger?" she whispered in my ear.

"You certainly do work fast," I whispered back.

"A girl's got to know what she wants and when to reach out and grab it," she said stressing her point by reaching between my legs and giving the family jewels a gentle, friendly squeeze.

Without another word Julie threw some bills on the bar, grabbed my hand and lead me out. She disappeared for a few minutes, coming back with a key and a six pack she must have picked up at the beer and wine store.

I'd like nothing more than to boast to myself how great the sex was with that beautiful stranger but that would be exaggerating to the point of lies. Truth is, once the door closed, Julie threw me up against a wall, virtually ripped my clothes off (which I in turn did to her), pushed and pulled each other onto the bed and explored each other a little more fully. All with a drunken, beer burp zeal.

If she looked beautiful clothed, she was gorgeous naked.

I was loaded. Very loaded. But my only saving grace was that Julie was just as tanked as I was.

We rolled around, my head spinning all the while.

Now it wasn't bad drunk sex—it was awful. But I had a great time and if her moans and shakes said anything I'm sure Julie did too. And it isn't that the booze caused me to climax too soon—

truth is the booze caused me to not orgasm at all.

Everything else was working great, Julie was worked up like only a beautiful, freshly divorced woman drunk in bed with a complete stranger could be worked up. But after close to an hour of various speeds, angles and positions Julie pushed me back saying with all sweetness, "you keep this up baby and you're either going to wear another hole in me or start a fire."

At first I wasn't quite sure what she was saying (room was still rotating) but then I realized my own nether-region was getting a little on the "frictioned" side too. Pulling out and rolling onto my side I gently kissed her nipple.

"You always like this?" she said pulling my head up to her face.

"What do you mean?" I said knowing what she was getting at but trying my hardest to hint that I was some kind of super-sex-man. In reality, parts of me were feeling like I'd peeled the skin off in little slivers. It hurt just to lay there.

"You know what I mean. Or are you just a man of supreme control."

I rolled over onto my back pulling her close to me, she put her head on my chest, running her long nails over my torso.

"Some things you just don't discuss."

She snort-snickered. "You mean kind of like a magician?"

"Sure. Anyway, you still had fun didn't you?" I said half afraid she was actually complaining.

Julie looked up at me, her long blond hair in rat's nests on her head. "Did you hear me complaining?"

I reached over to the nightstand beside the bed and grabbed another beer.

As the night made its way closer to the afternoon we lay in bed joking around, drinking more beer and fumbling around each other's bodies until we barely knew what we were doing anymore.

# Sight

When I woke up the next morning I was more than surprised that I wasn't hungover. My mind seemed crystal clear for a change.

I looked around at the room, our clothes thrown everywhere. I shook my head at myself. Never in my life would I have expected to be picked up and spend a day screwing some woman I didn't know.

The sheets smelled of sweat and beer. Julie was already in the shower.

After sitting in bed for a few minutes the shower turned off and the bathroom door opened.

I expected a "good morning" or at least "hello" but instead, "you're still here—I thought you'd have hit the road by now."

"Pardon." I said blinking.

"What were you hoping for, a screw in the shower? Or maybe a good-morning blowjob?"

She looked like Julie and sounded like her but she wasn't even looking at me while she was shouting, still drying her hair.

"Why are you looking so surprised? Did you really think it was going to be any different? I needed a good fuck and got an all right one. Now it's time for you to hit the road."

"I...I...I was just hoping..."

"Hoping you'd landed yourself a catch? Or just another ride?

Just get your fucking clothes and get out before I grab you by the balls and toss you out."

She went back into the bathroom and slammed the door.

I just sat there staring at the closed door for a couple minutes trying to process what had just happened. I didn't exactly expect a long term commitment from the woman but being tossed out the door by some deranged dominatrix was putting my brain on the road to system failure.

Moving one leg and then the other I wandered around the room bending and replacing my clothes.

I could hear her peeing in the bathroom humming to herself as she did.

Without saying a word I grabbed my stuff and silently went out the door and started looking for another ride. I didn't know if I should be pissed off, go back to the room and ask her "what the fuck is her problem" or maybe grab the keys to her car and take off. But instead I just wandered down the street to a truck stop I'd seen when we rolled into town the day before.

As I trudged down the highway I realized with a burning clarity that although she didn't want to acknowledge the day before, I had a souvenir that was more painful than a pain in the neck and far south of the border.

The gods who decide on the ride a hitchhiker is going to get must have left me after Julie. The first ride I got was from a very strange and very racist trucker named Stan. I didn't ride with him for long. I spent most of the day turning to stick out a thumb every time I heard a car as I hiked the highway by foot.

But eventually a good soul pulled over and picked me up, asking me to sit in the back seat of his huge white car. I never did get his name or any conversation. We just drove with country music blaring and then he pulled over when we got to Banff. I got out, bent over to say thanks or wave or something, but he just pulled back onto the highway and drove away.

Years earlier I'd been to Banff on a week-long camping trip. It was May—great lesson learned in just how cold it can get and how much snow is possible on a mountainside. It was the kind of trip that you never forget—and although at the time I'd never have admitted it, I had a great time.

It was terrific to be back. Despite a road-numb ass and legs (not to mention my sex-inflicted injury) I walked through the streets, remembering the sights and smells, and smiled to see that a number of the shops I remembered were still in business.

There aren't many places on earth like Banff—especially when you're viewing it from the bridge on your way to the big old hotel, looking back towards Mt. Rundle.

Massive investments had changed some of the town that I remembered and jazzed up others—but Banff will always be Banff—it has a feeling that is unique and magical.

Not quite ready for a review of my cold nights spent camping under the stars during my last stay, I headed for the youth hostel where I was sure I could trade some work for a bed since I was next to broke.

The hostel was much the way it was when I'd seen it last. A large institutional-type building—the trees around it were a little larger, a paint job had spruced things up a little but on the whole, everything was the same.

After a quick talk to the "guy in charge" it was agreed I'd clean all of the washrooms in exchange for a place to crash.

What I'd forgotten was that the beds were bunks and without mattresses or blankets.

So, as you can imagine, sleeping a night without blankets of any sort on top of a plywood board isn't the peak of human comfort. But it was warm and with my bag under my head and my coat thrown over me I managed to sleep well enough. Actually, to be honest, after walking most of the day and hardly sleeping the night before, I slept like the dead—and likely would have slept just as well on a bed of nails.

Beggars can't be choosers.

But when the next morning came I really knew what it felt like to have a pain in the neck...and the back, the shoulders, and just about every hair on my body. Needless to say, the first thing on my list of "to do" was to get myself a sleeping bag.

# Mountains

I didn't have any money, especially after I spent my last few dollars putting some breakfast in my gut—but when I was on the street in Vancouver I remembered some of the street crowd talking about going to social services and sometimes lucking out, that all you needed to do was get a nice social worker and a good story.

I'd never tried it before, but now with the prospect of begging coming into the picture again I decided to give it a try—worst they could do was say no.

So I cleaned myself up the best I could and put on the saddest face I could find, marched into the office, talked to a nice middle-aged woman, explained that I'd been in Banff for some time and hadn't found any work, had just got kicked out of the apartment I'd been sharing, and was broke.

Happy doesn't describe the feeling I walked away with. I threw in a few tears to beef up a pretty mediocre sob story. It felt awful to lie but it netted me the easiest money I'd ever seen in my life—emergency money she called it noting I could be put on welfare if I needed that down the road—and all I had to do was sell my soul. But I got over that part easily enough after picking myself up a new sleeping bag and some other provisions.

Of course now my name was in the system and if anyone had been or was still looking for me since my great escape I wouldn't be too hard to find—at least not while staying in Banff.

The thought had crossed my mind to give a false name but I knew well enough that the government wouldn't give you a dime unless they saw identification. Luckily, when I ran that day I had done so with my identification in a fanny pack.

It was a miserable feeling knowing that I'd virtually turned myself in thanks to the flag now attached to my name on some invisible digital highway. But the new gear and the change in my pocket felt good.

After picking up my new things and a quick trip back to the hostel to drop them off, I headed for the hills.

Last time I'd been in the park I spent most of my time poking around in the backcountry, hiking through the woods and scrambling up mountainsides or riding down rivers of loose shale. Being back in the same bush felt great—strangely warm and secure. From the hoodoos, Stoney Squaw, Mt. Rundle, the trees, magpies and on and on—this was the best place on earth to me. Even when the clouds made the day grey it felt as if the sun was shining. For the first time in a very long while everything seemed all right. As I wandered along the familiar trails that hadn't really changed at all in the years since I'd been gone I wished silently to myself that I could stay forever.

But as I hiked under a circling eagle silently watching me from above I knew full well that my days were limited in this place that was a heaven but not a haven. Soon enough there would be people asking me questions or someone remembering my face from a missing poster—all these questions had answers I didn't want to even start dreaming up.

Ahead of me I could hear some shouting and looked through the trees to see coloured ropes dangling from a crag on the side of a low mountain. The ropes were jerking under some climber's movements—seeing the brightly-coloured threads instantly brought a smile to my face bringing back memories of a time that now seemed very far off.

Trying my best to not run, I headed straight for the climbers.

There was a group of them—a climbing club as I'd find out —all waiting their turn for a try on the top-roped pitch.

As I got closer I could see that the route they were fighting their way up was pretty rough looking and you could see they were having a good challenge getting up.

One 30-ish woman in tights and a big wool sweater was standing back from the rest, quietly watching, taking in the climber's efforts from a full-view perspective.

"Hi there," I said coming up beside her.

"Hi, how you doing?" she smiled quickly looking over at me and then back at the rock slab.

"Great day for a climb."

"Sure is, the rock's a little cold but the sun's out and warming it up. Even cold rock climbing is better than no climbing," she said.

"I know what you mean."

She looked over at me. "Do you climb?"

I looked over at the progress of the climbers and shrugged. "I haven't been climbing much lately but yeah—I live for it."

She looked back at the crag too.

"Think you'd like to give it a go? I'm sure I could borrow a harness for you and I know some of the guys have extra shoes with them," she raised an eyebrow.

I knew full well that I was out of shape but seeing that eyebrow raised made me feel like she was daring me and I've always been the type to never turn down a dare.

"Would l ever like to climb. That would be so great."

As we walked over to the group of people standing with heads looking skyward under the overhang we introduced ourselves and Sarah (as she told me to call her) went right to work. In no time she had hunted up everything I'd need.

My face was starting to hurt from all of the grinning I realized I was doing. And it felt great.

No sooner had I tied in (on a little easier route than the other climbers were hauling up), shouted out, "climbing," and started up, that I realized with a sudden and clear understanding just how out of shape I'd become.

I only got a few arms lengths up the slab of rock and my arms and legs were shaking with effort, my body dripping with sweat, and my heart felt like it was going to bounce right out of my chest.

But somehow I struggled on.

As the rock bit into my fingertips I couldn't help but think about St. Joseph continuing on even though everyone thought he was a dolt or some sort of spawn of the devil instead of a divinely inspired innocent.

Of course St. Joseph would have been able to fly up the rock—backwards—but I was pulling and pushing with great effort. And as shitty as I was doing I once again marvelled to myself on the way up—using my chin on holds to ease up the work on my trembling and tired arms and legs—at how God must have made mountains for humans to climb. Each arm length of rock gave out its secret hand holds—all in the perfect place, right where I'd put them myself if I was making the wall.

After what felt like much more time than had really passed I pushed myself up to the top and looked down to the cheering, smiling faces.

There are few people on earth as happy and carefree as true climbers. Maybe it has something to do with the fact they take a chance with life and death every time they haul up a crag, putting reality into perspective.

Feeling content despite my poor showing I leaned back in the harness letting the gear support me—always the hardest part of any climb. The idea of trusting your belayer completely, or your bunch of man-made gear, has always left a grain of festering doubt in my mind. At least when I was climbing my life was in my arms, legs and ability—coming down (unless you were down-climbing) depends totally on trust.

With all this going through my mind, my feet touched back on mother earth. Silently I thanked God, all the Bodhisattvas in the universe, and the good green rope I'd just been umbilically attached to—then I turned, smiling at Sarah who'd been my belayer.

"You look like you've had a great time."

"Ah, that's because I did—man that was great," I said only slightly fibbing and then realized as I turned back to look up at the pitch I'd just climbed that I really did have a great time despite the work and my limbs that were still quivering.

"The only problem is that I'm so out of shape and this proved it."

"You looked like you know your rock from this angle," she grinned at me.

"Sure—from this angle all you could see was my ass, which pretty much sums up my competence level on that climb."

Sarah laughed, grabbed me by the shoulder, spinning me around. "You're right about watching your ass—and you really need to know there is nothing wrong with that part of you at all."

Blood was rising to my cheeks. At first I looked down at my feet but then glanced up at her and grinned back.

It was one of those moments that you could live a lifetime in. Everything slowed.

But just as I was falling into the well to her soul, another climber wandered over and slapped me on the back.

"Hey man, that climb wasn't bad. You're really flexible—looked like a spider crawling up there."

Not wanting to get back into the humble pie, I just nodded and said, "thanks."

I turned my attention back to Sarah who was bending over pulling her harness off.

"Talking about asses," I said without thinking.

She turned her head, looking back at me smiling, "you getting a nice look?"

I started to feel really stupid for my comment (which was possibly be the dumbest thing I'd ever said), but she grinned and bent over more, content in fixing up her gear knowing I was watching—not minding that I was watching.

And if she didn't mind me watching I wasn't going to act like I minded the view. Things were looking good.

# Knowing

After a stop at a pub to share a pitcher or two, the conversation flowed much easier.

Sarah had been living in Banff for the past year after taking off from her hometown in Ontario in search of adventure.

She said that one day riding the bus home from work she saw an ad for the big hotel that is the epicentre of Banff displayed in a photo spread in a magazine. Two days later she was hitchhiking her way west.

"I don't know what it was about those pictures. Something just snapped I guess."

I smiled back at her from the other side of the table.

"Do you think I'm nuts?" she said gulping back the bottom of a pint. "I mean leaving a job, a boyfriend, family—all for a picture in a glossy magazine?"

I picked up my glass of beer and looked at the bubbles rolling up through the liquid amber feeling like a king tasting the very best of the world. I took a long drink and wiped my face with a sleeve, shaking my head as I swallowed.

"No. I think that was probably the single most sane thing you could have done with your life. Too often we look over all the great things in life, the real taste of your beer, bubbles moving through liquid, God in the movement of a woman's hips."

Sarah looked at me and slowly grinned. "What do you

mean?" She slid her hand across the table, first lightly touching my fingers then grabbing my hand.

"Have you enjoyed your life here?"

She nodded, "it has been great—I love it here."

"Then I'd have to say you did the right thing. Any moment in life where we really live we're doing the right thing. Every time we delude ourselves we're wrong."

She gripped my hand harder. We just sat there smiling at each other. I half expected her to let out a belch and start laughing at my insight. But instead she smiled and the universe seemed to expand around me—I know what God must have felt like during the Big Bang.

Before long Sarah's flirtatious hand holding became leg rubbing. It was becoming obvious we had more in common than a destiny to run away and end up in Banff.

I couldn't help but laugh inside at the fact I seemed to have some sort of woman magnet on me, musing that it took becoming a junkie and dropping out of the world to become attractive. Maybe I was just attracting women who wanted someone to nurture—or maybe they just wanted what all of us really want, someone to hold and forget about the moment with.

After a few hours of playing footsy and draining our share of pitchers we were wandering down the street, arm-in-arm. Actually, wandering wasn't the best word to describe our walk. We were drunk and needed each other to keep upright.

And as happens when inhibitions are loosened thanks to a brew or seven—Sarah and I were all over each other.

Laughing, staggering drink-drunk she lead me through Banff—I was way beyond lost.

"So, where are you taking me or are you abducting me?"

"I am abducting you and plan to hold you for ransom at my place," she said punching me in the arm, nearly knocking us both ass over tea kettle into the street.

"I have to warn you—I don't have any money to pay ransom. And my family thinks I'm dead."

"That's OK, I'm sure you and I can figure out another form of payment," she said grabbing my hand and pulling me up some steps to a small apartment she said was her place.

The key barely out of the lock and the door not yet totally open, Sarah was already tugging at my pants. I giggled, not quite sure how to take this woman.

"And what exactly do you think you're doing?"

"I think you know—and if you don't I'll show you soon enough."

She closed the door, leaning against it looking wide-eyed with a big-toothed grin.

"So what happens now?" I said taking a step back.

"Now I take off this shirt," she said flinging it at me quicker than I could even process her taking it off. "And now these pants."

I don't think my jaw hit the floor but then again my mind wasn't really focused on things like jaw movement.

She walked past me, running her hand up the inside of my leg.

"And now I'm going to have a shower—you are going to drop those clothes you have on right where you stand and follow me," she ordered.

I turned, watching her dancer's body move perfectly in the dim light.

"You really are a woman who knows what she wants," I said watching her move towards the bathroom. When she was out of sight I heard the shower starting up.

"I know exactly what I want—and you had better be dropping your drawers and joining me."

Without any more prodding I unbuckled my belt.

Steam was already billowing out of the bathroom's open door when I left my clothing piled in a heap.

Behind the frosted glass of the shower door I could see she was running her hands over her skin. She was beautiful.

I thought back to Jo and my pledge to her that I was going to be some sort of wandering Zen monk of the new millennium—right now I seemed about as far from religious experience as I could get.

"You know, God made these body parts for a reason," I mumbled to myself.

"What was that?"

"Nothing."

She opened the shower door, hair wet.

"You sure are slow," her eyes were taking a slow slide over my body. She wasn't ashamed to let me know she was taking a good look at the full package.

"Slow but sure," I said. "Don't forget that story about the tortoise and the hare."

Grabbing me by the arm and pulling me to her lips, one hand grabbing my ass, she pulled me into the shower. "I don't want to talk anymore. Just shut up."

The hot water ran over us as we kissed, our hands exploring each other.

She moved her hand down over my stomach and grabbed a hold of me, squeezing softly. I could feel myself throbbing.

Turning her back to me, she pushed me into her warmth.

While my mind was screaming, my lips were tasting the salt on the skin of her back and shoulders, my hands feeling the firm nipples of her breasts and neatly trimmed triangle of hair near the place where she gently reached back between her legs, guiding me deeper inside of her.

It was like smooth heaven. With each thrust came visions of

Mary, the strange blond woman, shooting up, Ginger dead, public service announcements against unsafe sex—but nothing mattered. All there was in those slowed moments was the simple gift from God in the perfection of our bodies moving together, joined as one, with water and steam dancing around us.

In a nearly painful explosion I came—panting, cheek pressed against her shoulder, a hand clutching her breast.

She moaned.

Her hands moved down over mine, moving them both down to that wet warmth, slowly, then more rapidly delving into her.

Soon, in a rolling shudder we found the right spot. Like an electrical current suddenly turned on I could swear I saw a flash of light. We both groaned, our bodies quivering together.

Sarah reached out to steady herself, putting her hands on the walls of the shower, took a deep breath, arching her back.

We stood there, hot water raining down on us.

"Oh, so that's what you had in mind," I said smiling from ear to ear.

Brushing wet hair back from her face she looked back at me, "yeah, something like that."

"I don't know about you but I need to lie down," I said still clutching her in my arms, my legs shaking.

"You know, I think you've got the biggest perma-grin I've ever seen?"

"You don't look so sad yourself," I said as my legs began to buckle and I decided just to sit on the floor of the shower, the water feeling like a mothers touch on my face. Sarah leaned over—grabbing a wrist I pulled her down to me.

As we kissed I opened my eyes, watching steam surrounding us, rising from the water and our bodies. I couldn't help but wish that time could just stop dead in this moment—but it didn't.

# Mornings

Sarah and I spent two days together—mostly in bed. While we had sex until sore, we also spent a fair amount of time talking climbing and philosophy.

As it turned out, not only was Sarah a great climber and a dominate woman but she was also a philosophy junkie with a particular addiction to Socrates. In the middle of a conversation on just about anything, she'd slide in a sidebar on Socrates' view on whatever it was we were talking about—or at least what she expected Socrates would have thought.

There were a few times I was about to pipe up and tell her about St. Joseph of Copertino but for one of the first times in my life I literally told myself to shut up and just listen to what someone else was trying to tell me. She had some great insights—it felt great to be able to sit, talk and not have to worry about anything.

I just sat back and smiled, listening. I couldn't remember the last time I'd had such a good time or such great and spontaneous conversation.

But while she openly told me of her life and views on everything, I evaded personal questions, telling her only that I was kind of on the run. She smirked and told me she knew from first sight that I was "a bad seed."

I laughed hard, one of those gut-muscle tearing guffaws.

Eventually I pulled myself together and told her I had to get back to the hostel where I had a deal worked out and my stuff was stored.

"You can stay with me," she said still naked, watching me dress.

I turned my head, jumping on one foot while trying to get my other leg into my pants.

"I'd love to stay here with you but you have a job and I've got stuff I need to look after," I lied not wanting to tell her what I really was thinking about was hitting the road.

"Look, why don't you get your stuff from the hostel and come back here—I have plenty of room. If sharing my bed is so bad there's always the couch," she said slyly pulling the covers up to her chin.

I had to admit it made a lot of sense. And I could think of about a million places on the earth I'd rather sleep than a room filled with bunks of snoring strangers—it felt a little too much like my time back on the street in Vancouver.

"Okay but remember, I'm not here to stay—I have to get back on the road eventually," I said in a voice almost begging—mostly with myself.

"If you really want to do what you say you have to I understand," she said from the bed. "Let's just spend what time we can with each other though."

I nodded. "I guess that wouldn't be too bad."

Sarah threw a pillow at me from across the room, hitting me in the face. I tossed it back.

"Get out of here now and get your things. I'll leave a key under the pot outside. I'll expect to see you back here in this bed tonight."

Without much thought I wandered to the edge of the bed, bent and kissed her, brushing hair from her face. "I'll see you in a little while. Have a good time at work."

I started to turn and walk towards the door but stopped and turned back, "thank you."

She smiled saying nothing.

Leaving her exactly how I wanted to remember her I headed for the hostel across town.

After two days of basically staying in bed or lounging around Sarah's apartment, it felt weird to be out and about. The world seemed to be moving in high gear.

Once I got to the hostel it took no time at all to realize there had been people—likely cops—asking questions about me. No one said anything to me about it but in the way they looked at me, especially the people behind the desk,  I just had to get out of there.

I'd known giving my name to social services would be an invitation to questioning. The problem of course would be that either the police would think I was me or they'd think I was my murderer using my identification to get some easy money.

If I didn't watch it I'd be answering all the questions I'd been avoiding all this time—I've never been the type that likes answering questions, or talking to cops.

Without wasting time I headed to my room, hoping all my stuff was still there and luckily I wasn't disappointed. It looked like it had been gone through but everything was there. Packaging it all up, I hoisted it onto my back and headed out the back door.

Using every back alley and hedge I could find I made for the trails that surround Banff (better to leave creating more questions than give hints at answers).

As I trudged through the woods I went over my options, from hitching for a ride to camping out. But all ended with being found out and forced to make some sort of restitution for abandoning a wife and dropping off the edge of the earth. That is, I went through all the options except sneaking back to Sarah's and hiding out until I could get on the road without eyes watching around me.

I wandered around for a little while, enjoying the freedom that the woods around Banff radiated. Sitting on a rock looking up at the blue sky I decided with nod that I'd rather stay in these parts for a while, poke around in the woods, find out what really goes on inside a person's head—and a warm inviting bed with a beautiful woman wasn't something to scoff at either. At least for the time being.

Truth was, as long as I was going to continue running I'd have to do it with the understanding the longer I stayed in any one place the easier it would be that someone would notice me, or my name would turn up bringing police and questioning.

I felt a sense of shame for having left Mary but I also knew I was doing all of this for some reason hidden to me. Like a medieval knight on a quest I was being lead by an ethereal hand to the road, bearing witness to the labours of man and paying for the sins of the world. I knew how bizarre it sounded thinking these thoughts to myself but for the first time in my life I knew I was doing the right thing. I thought of the Bodhisattva stories Jo had told me and knew in my heart that the secret underlying essence was that I had to go moan in the wilderness. I could hear the haunting tone of a lost voice in the void chanting, "go, go, go...go for the sick and go for the sane...go for the young and go for the old...go...go..."

Looking up at the clouds hovering with ever changing movements I decided that my life was going to be much different from this point. No one else would ever understand truly what I was doing or why but I had to go.

The world seemed suddenly much brighter than it had ever been. I looked at my hands feeling, almost hearing the blood sliding through my veins—what a mystery that they are even there, moving with instantaneous thought.

Watching a magpie land, pick something up and leave I suddenly realized that our lives actually run in reverse, each moment a goodbye, a sacred gift that we don't appreciate until we realize that it is really and forever gone.

I understood why Jo said to me in my fevered withdrawal that the secret to enlightenment is sitting. The action of searching is futile since the moment you take your first step you are already losing time, and more life than you'll ever know.

A raven taunted me from a tree above, bringing me back from the veil of transcendental reality I'd somehow spontaneously breached.

Making sure no-one was following or had been watching me I stood and found my way back to Sarah with the voice still vibrating into my marrow and far beyond, "...go...go...go!"

# Daze

While she had a job and had to take off from time to time we spent the next week mostly getting to know each other better.

And while we had our passionate moments we spent a lot of time talking about life in general.

Then one night after making love, Sarah turned to me and asked the question I knew would come eventually. One that no one, not even myself had really asked all of this time and the moment it rattled through my mind visions of Mary, Mojo, Jo, and the open road all came to life in front of me.

"What are you doing?"

"What do you mean, I'm just lying here." I said, knowing exactly what she was getting at. The phantom images just hovered around her waiting for an answer.

"I mean what are you running from? I think I know you well enough to know you couldn't hurt a fly so I think I know you haven't killed anyone. So what is it? What are you doing?"

Feeling uneasy and somewhat claustrophobic I sat up rigid in bed.

Sarah grabbed my arm. "Don't think you're going any-where. I mean you've been sharing my bed and my place—I think I deserve some kind of story. Especially since I know full well one of these days I'm going to come home and you'll be gone."

I looked at her desperately wanting to tell her something she'd want to hear. Anything but the truth we both knew. But instead, reaching out into the thin air, grabbing for a good lie, I came back with the truth.

"I...I don't think I really know," I said holding the sides of my head sobbing silently. "I don't know what I'm doing. I just started running a long time ago and I haven't been able to stop—I just have to keep running."

Sarah sat in the darkness looking at me, her hand still holding my arm.

"Have you ever been somewhere or done something you've felt so bad about—almost like every force on earth was trying to, screaming at you to get out, to leave?"

"Yeah, I think I have," she said quietly. "I've been on climbs I just knew were bad news—the feeling is usually right."

I snorted back tears. "Well, make that feeling about a million times stronger. Make that feeling tell you that you want to, you have to get out of your own life, your own skin—that's what I have felt like for a very long time. To be honest I don't even remember how long. Christ, most of the time I don't even remember who I am anymore. I just want out—out of this pointless, fake life."

She loosened her grip, rubbing her hand on my arm. "If you don't like your life you can change it—you don't have to hide out and run just for the sake of running," she said softly.

I shook my head slowly. "You don't understand, no one does—that's the problem." My whole body was shaking and shuddering with each breath and sob. "When you climb all that matters is the next hold. All those fake bullshit masks we wear fall off the edge and tumble away. What you're left with is reality—all that matters is right now. All that matters is this breath. All that matters is continuing the climb, getting to the top. Everything else is just bullshit that will fuck up your life, make you miss what you should be grabbing for and kill you."

I could hear the clock in the other room ticking.

"That's what I'm running from—the fact that this life is just bullshit."

Sarah put an arm around me, trying to pull me closer to her. "You don't really believe that do you?"

She was waiting for another answer.

"And if I do? What if I told you I left my family, friends, a good job—all because I saw with clear eyes one day after coming down from a mountain. Don't you ever sit awake...have you ever looked into the face of someone you love and realized that even though this face means the world to you, if you don't die first, you'll live to see this perfect moment, this person that means a universe to you, and everyone else you know...they're all going to die, die and leave you alone? Can you imagine how empty the world can really get? Can you see a world where you are just by yourself and all that is left of this reality you hold so close to you right now is distant memories that you can't even know if they are real or images you've dreamt up to replace the empty holes that your mind has paved over?"

Images of the dark, echoing house the night before I made my run flashed through my mind. And further back, to a time I didn't want to remember when the echoes didn't shake the windows of that small house, a time when Mary was full of life, I was full of life and we both knew how to smile.

I bit the inside of my lip hard, doing my best to relock the doors that were opening. I could taste the warm coppery taste of blood, it gave me some comfort.

Sarah wasn't saying anything and I noticed she had pulled her arm away from me.

"Maybe I'm not running from anything—maybe I'm running towards something, something I don't even know. Maybe I run because it is all I can do to keep from disappearing. Maybe I run because when I'm doing it I know that at that moment I am alive."

While I couldn't see her in the darkness I could hear that she was crying now. I didn't realize it at the time but I had been screaming at her all this time through my tears.

After a few minutes of the two of us sitting, crying in silence, she said quietly, "I guess if you don't want to hear the answer you shouldn't ask the question."

"I'm sorry Sarah. I didn't mean to shout...it's just..."

"Don't worry about it," she said getting out of bed. "But I think it might be for best if you headed out tomorrow—I care too much about you now to wait around to see what you're going to do next, whether you're going to kill yourself or just disappear."

I reached out for her. "Sarah, I..."

"No," she pulled back from me standing up and going to the window. "Everything you said is what you feel or maybe it's what you don't feel. But I don't really think there is a place for me, or us in there—I just don't know."

There really was nothing left for me to say. I just sat there like a fool, wiping tears off my face, watching as she left the room, snapping on a light in the livingroom.

Sarah was right. No answer I could give to her would help. Nothing I could say would have lessened the impact of what I had just screamed at her.

That she was frightened, I could understand perfectly—I felt the same way most of the time since that morning when I decided to keep running.

And now it was the only thing I knew how to do. I had to get back on the road.

# Out

Before the sun was showing itself over the mountain peaks I'd already thrown together what gear I had and snuck out the door.

Sarah was sound asleep on the couch, a blanket clutched in her arms.

I wanted to—or at least thought about—leaving a note of thanks. But I vetoed the idea. What would thanks get me anyway? I knew and she would know a note was just more of an elaborate con—a note would be just anther ritual, a mask in the same web of bullshit I'd just lectured about.

So instead, I silently closed the door behind me and put my shoes on outside, hoisting the sleeping bag I'd rolled up with my scant belongings, tied up neatly with a short length of climbing rope, threw it over my shoulder and marched on.

Although I told myself that I'd been mostly using Sarah—as she'd likely been using me—I did have some fun. If I had left a note, I'd probably have written only a few words, but golden ones that brought a grin to my face just thinking about them: "I smiled. It felt good."

As I turned down another street heading for the highway I looked back at her place wondering if she was still asleep, wondering what she'd feel at seeing me gone, wondering what kind of future she had and what it could have been like if things had been different for us.

But they weren't. And I wasn't.

I turned my back on those thoughts, readjusted my roll with a bit of a hop and headed toward the highway traffic—I could already hear racing in two directions, people headed to something or somewhere. I couldn't help but think back to Sarah, Jo and Mary, knowing at least some of these people zooming down the highway were headed to someone. But those people weren't me. And for the first time I had a clear understanding that I really was headed nowhere. And it was all right. Knowledge, even if it is some strange reverse knowledge, still brings a calm feeling.

Standing on the edge of the highway, watching cars, campers and trucks zooming by I was hit with the irony that while I might be okay with my trek along the road to nowhere, I still had to head in one direction or another—and I didn't know which way to go.

But luckily I didn't have to worry about that for long. As I stood there on the edge of the highway trying to feel which way the wind was blowing, a van pulled up, window rolled down and a head popped out.

The head held a face that looked almost clown-like with the biggest grin I'd ever seen. And despite the scruffy look and long unkept hair I knew this guy wasn't going to rob me. A cloud of smoke, with that unmistakable scent of marijuana billowed out of the open window and into my face—or more precisely, right up my nose.

"Hey guy—you wanna ride?"

I looked into the van, past the dangling fuzzy dice to see another smiling face—this one, while just as scruffy, was much rounder, reminding me of those big round yellow happy faces you see everywhere. The smoke in the van was thick, a cloud you could just about cut with a knife, or better yet, try to put into a bottle to save until later.

I smiled back at them wondering to myself at what part of the night it becomes morning—and too early to get stoned.

I looked down the highway which was strangely now empty.

The van rumbled in front of me, smoke still warmly billowing out of the windows.

A magpie screamed somewhere behind me, I started to look for it but was interrupted.

"So, you wanna ride man?" the happy-faced driver said.

"Which way you going?" I asked grinning back.

He looked over at his buddy (or maybe they were brothers, lovers, criminals on the run), shrugged. "We're just headed this way—wanna come?"

The magpie screamed at me again.

I looked either way down the long highway, still empty.

Knowing it could very easily be a long time before I met a pair as harmless as these two, I opened the side door and rolled into the back of the van, pulling my gear with me, saying, "sure, I'd love to."

Dwight and Logan introduced themselves before I'd even closed the door and the van was put into gear. They were of that breed of young people who for some reason think 1967 was more than just the creation of concert promoters and assorted others. While their parents willingly outgrew the 60's, their children went right back.

Watching them share another joint (I didn't want to know how many they'd had in the past few hours—mostly because I dreaded the answer), listening to the Grateful Dead over the van's stereo, I couldn't help but laugh inside—and it had nothing to do with the pot. Well, maybe a little.

These hippies of the turn of the century were something else. Just as fake as the Mohawk-wearing punk or Vespa-riding mod, the thousand dollar suit, or the hairy feminist—all were just more of these masks, attempts at trying to fit into a world without much meaning and no real answers to all the obvious questions about what "all this" was about.

I can remember times when I'd sit watching these new millennium poser-hippies with their self-absorbed noses in the air trying to act like the best hippie they could muster from borrowed images of this movie or that documentary. Or maybe they actually picked their act up from seeing some God-forsaken deadheads who miraculously remained stoned through the 70s, 80s and 90s and would likely stay stoned for the rest of their lives oblivious to the passing of time.

I remember meeting a guy when I first moved to the Sunshine Coast (one of the last remaining havens for these 60s hangers-on) who had decided he was moving. When I asked why he was pulling up stakes and travelling on his answer was simple, "too many fucking hippies." A newcomer to the area I didn't know if he was serious or not—to be honest up until that point I don't think I'd ever so much as seen a hippie except for some long haired people I drove past who were hitchhiking at the side of the highway in Salmon Arm years earlier. I had no idea what a group of supposedly peace-loving, back-to-earth type of people could do to get someone's back-hairs up on end so much that they needed to get away.

But now I understood.

They were hippies, not as a sign or reflection of the times, but of themselves. They were wearing costumes in a vain attempt to create their own reality, oblivious to the fact that the rest of the world (including most of the original 60s hippies) had moved on and thought of them as freaks.

But hey, at least (as I was finding out first hand) they shared their smoke.

We drove—I lost track of how long—Dwight was driving way below the speed limit and as they lit up seemingly joint after joint his driving ability wasn't improving. But I was beginning to care less and less.

There was virtually no conversation, just the usual pot-talk and the occasional, "hey, don't hog that roach." Eventually I decided I'd rather rough it walking than end up crashed into a ditch or over a bridge in a smoke-filled van, meeting my maker with Cheech and Chong. So I figured I'd best hop out and hike it alone for a while. It would be safer and my eyes were killing me from the smoke—not to mention that I felt way too stoned for a morning that I had expected to be full of clarity of action.

Without any argument, Dwight pulled the van over beside a mountain creek. I shook their hands, thanked them for the ride and headed back out the way I came in, only this time with a head that was spinning. I was sure I'd fall out of the van. But I didn't. And as I turned to close the van door Logan reached back, eyes looking painfully red. "Here man, if you get cold tonight, smoke this—you'll still be cold but you won't mind it as much—you'll be too interested watching the wind and listening to the stars."

Trying to keep my equilibrium I said thanks and put the joint into my pocket, waved goodbye, closed the door and stood back, watching them drive away.

Needing to come back to reality a little before looking for another ride I headed down the embankment to the grey-white coloured water of the mountain creek.

# Rush

After finding the perfect butt-sized boulder I carefully padded my 100 per cent natural rock chair with my bedroll so as not to get haemorrhoids (at least that's what my childhood Scout leader warned us of, "always put something under your butt if you sit on a rock or you'll get piles." I didn't know if it was good advice or not but I took it and followed it most of my life.)

Then I just sat.

There were a few little bits and pieces of food in my gear that I'd brought along and I munched some of them while watching the creek washing by over the round rocks of its bed.

While the water was greyish it still had a clean feeling to it—and how could it not in this mountain paradise. I looked around myself with jagged mountains towering like teeth of some massive beast growling around me.

Not wanting to completely eat myself out of house and home (so to speak), I soon decided I'd eaten enough and wanted to explore the woods on my side of the creek since I didn't really have anything else to do and no appointments on my agenda.

While I was only a stone's throw from the busy Trans Canada Highway, the woods were seriously thick, taking more than a passing effort to dig my way into them.

But a hundred or so feet into the woods, travel became a lot easier as the bigger trees took over from the small scrub and brambles at the edge.

This was the kind of place you see on documentaries about great parks—it was amazing. Moss grew proudly on the sides of some of the most naturally beautiful trees I'd ever seen. It was like heaven. Birds were singing and I could still hear the rumble of the white water in the creek.

It's embarrassing to admit, but poking around in the woods, watching where I was placing my feet more than what was in front of me, I literally bumped into a small log shack that some trapper, miner or prospector had built a long time ago.

It was small with weathered grey wood and a roof of twigs that had almost totally caved in.

Seeing the cabin brought a child-like joy that made me feel almost like I was shining—instantly excited.

The moment I saw the cabin I knew what I was going to do tomorrow, and the day after, and the day after that.

Quickly I scrambled through the bush, ripping my skin on brambles as I tore through a little too excitedly. I ran over the creekbed to my gear which was still sitting exactly where I'd left it. The highway a couple hundred yards away was rumbling with traffic. I smiled to myself realizing I couldn't hear or see any cars from the cabin.

My cabin.

Gathering up the things into a bundle, I headed back for the path I'd already started to wear through the bush.

I couldn't help but grin as I got back to the shack and dropped all my stuff at the door.

With my hands on my hips and my chest jutting out I decided that this must be the place I'd been headed for all this time—like how ducks know exactly where to migrate to. I had been drawn to this cabin and I was going to be a modern day Walden, minus the pond.

Ever since I read Thoreau's Walden in high school, I'd harboured a secret dream of going it alone in the woods. Self-sufficient, just living life the way it was meant to be lived. And now I had my chance.

I slowly walked around the small weathered cabin, checking its condition, which turned out to be not all that bad for a building likely not by human eyes for the better part of a century. Apart from the roof which would need to be replaced, the rest just needed some pretty radical cleaning.

Inside was another story. Small trees were growing up from the old dirt floor, trying their best to make their way through some of the larger holes in the caved-in roof.

Not wanting to waste time I started cleaning out the interior of the shack, pulling out what remained of the roof. Soon I saw that once it was cleaned and rebuilt there would be just enough room to stand inside.

Deciding that replacing the roof would have to wait I went to work yanking out weeds and small trees from around and inside the cabin and when that was done and things were a little less chaotic than they had been, I started to further dismantle the roof, picking away at parts of the wall to be absolutely certain my new home wouldn't fall in on me in my sleep.

To my joy, most of the main beams of the cabin's roof were still usable.

It was hard work but it was joyous. I couldn't help but think about that Zen of work ethic Jo always pushed. This was work I could really get my teeth into. And knowing the end result of my efforts made me even more focused.

# Shelter

It wasn't much but it was mine—or at least for the time being, as I thought to myself silently thanking the brave soul who'd ingeniously built the structure back when there were no roads or lumber stores.

An early morning trip to a truck stop after a blissful evening sleeping under the stars inside my 10 foot by 10 foot box, brought me a trade of work for a blue tarp and enough provisions to last me a good while.

While I didn't want to tell the world where I was, after a night looking up at the stars I realized fast that I'd need a better roof than twigs and leaves alone.

And once I had the beams back in the homes they'd known all those years ago and fastened my new blue tarp over them, secured with a few good sized branches and a rock or two from the creek—I was pleased. The blue tarp gave a wild blue light to the inside of the cabin. It was great.

But my pride and joy were the bed and small table I'd made out of scavenged materials. The bed was mostly made of branches and a pile of super-soft moss I'd found, covered with a number of armfuls of leaves I'd gathered and my sleeping bag thrown on top—it was a little lumpy but it felt good knowing I'd made it myself. And as I'd soon find, I had never slept as well as I would on that bed.

And as for the table, it was a "construction ahead" sign I'd found discarded on the side of the highway, set on top of four good-sized boulders. It was a table that I thought would likely be the envy of any interior designer who saw it.

It was home sweet home—minus the sign proclaiming so over the door, so that too I took onto myself, carving it with a pocket knife I picked up the same time I bought my sleeping bag in Banff.

After a little more work I cleaned up the "front yard"—making a fire pit just outside the door and gathering a good pile of wood.

With the bulk of the work done, I settled down by a freshly set fire, cooking a fish freshly caught from the creek with some fishing line and gear I'd picked up with the tarp.

The fire crackling softly and the woods growing dark, I sat back relaxed. Looking around at my little blue-roofed shack I nodded my head—I'd done good.

Sometimes in life you're given small pleasures that keep you grinning from ear to ear. This cabin, as pathetic as it was, was just one of those pleasures. And I was more proud of it and with myself for the work I'd done on it than I'd ever been in my life.

At that moment I could see myself staying there for all eternity, cooking fish over an open fire only steps away from my simple, very human home.

What more could anyone dream of—I had food for my stomach, shelter from the elements and the natural, real world for my soul.

And while I was only a stone's throw from the rest of the world—that other world—I was also in my own new reality, a fresh step in my own personal evolution. And it felt great.

As I gazed into the glowing embers of the perfect fire I thought about all the people in all those homes that my neighbour, the highway, led to.

I couldn't feel anything but pity for those fools locked in mortgages for huge dwellings full of things they didn't need, addicted to that glowing box they all sat around every night, mindlessly staring at.

Safe and warm by my fire I wept for the delusion and suffering of the world. And I promised myself, pledging an oath with the creek, the woods, the fire, the open sky, and the mountains sitting silently buddha-like as my witnesses that I was going to live in my shack, away from all the falseness and lies of the world, for the sake of all those who couldn't see the truth. I was going to do it for all of those, working wandering drones, oblivious to the suffering in their own lives, and the suffering they were causing, and the suffering around them. Life as they knew it was not the way it was meant to be, reality was all messed up.

I looked deep into the flames wishing its purity could burn away all the delusion and bring true understanding to everyone. But I knew better. I knew that some people are and always have been destined for a life with blinders on. But for me things were different. Much different.

My mind raced back to that day on the side of the mountain, seeing the world with new eyes for the first time. It came so easily, just one ripple after another in a constant wave in an ocean that carried me all the way to this fire.

And while I knew that life was not what we'd conditioned ourselves into believing it was, I didn't pretend to know all the answers. I knew I was just as fucked up as the next guy—but I was getting better.

The unfortunate part of seeing a glimpse of the truth is the great cavernous hole it leaves afterwards. A part of me wished I'd been given a choice, like Alice, to either eat this pill and grow big or eat that pill and grow small—see the true picture or see another view of this ongoing falseness. It was a very lonely feeling seeing something nobody else could see, or at least seeing something that nobody else wants to admit seeing.

But then there was that other part of me that was happy to be living in the now with a clarity that set me apart and gave me the courage, if that's what it was, to run and keep running. And strangely enough, a part of my run seemed to be happening for all of those around me—while I was running away I was also running for them since they wouldn't do it themselves, or at least weren't willing to.

It was at those moments when I felt like Terry Fox, out on a lonely stretch of highway running for all those who couldn't run even though the pain was staggering. Maybe it was this pain, knowing there was something deep down below the surface of these feelings that kept the legs moving—a silent knowing.

I shook my head and pushed the logs in the fire sending up a dazzling cloud of sparks.

No, the wheel that started in motion long ago had brought me to this beautiful spot, removed and yet strangely connected with the world outside. This forest retreat of mine was meant as a sign. Or so I told myself in that dark void under mountains and trees lit only by my small fire, feeling like the last man in the world—or at least the last person striving to find meaning out of all of this stuff everyone else calls life.

I remembered reading something at Jo's about Buddhist monks who practised a renunciation that takes place in the bush. Thai forest monasticism I thought it was called, where monks choose to practise a naturalist dharma because Shakyamuni Buddha was born under a tree, became enlightened under a tree and died under a tree.

It sounded perfect to me.

With this way of uniting with the wilderness as a means of

becoming enlightened I decided that if was going to live the forest bhikkhu life I'd better start some sort of meditation practice.

But all of that could wait until morning—if I remembered anything about all those Zen books I'd devoured, it was to live in the moment. And in this moment I was just happy to be doing what I was doing—absolutely nothing beside a shack in the woods in front of a glowing, crackling fire.

# Kick start

Starting any new routine is tough—at least this is exactly what I told myself.

Waking up in the early blue-lit morning, I sat up in my soft, lumpy bed and looked up at the blue tarp, then down at my hands that looked the same colour in the defused light.

Sitting the way Jo taught me to meditate—I sat still, my back straight, eyes unfocused, just sitting, breathing, not thinking and not trying not to think.

Then a thought popped into my mind—just a small one but disruptive nonetheless—just how long was I supposed to sit like this?

Time started to feel like it was dragging on.

I started counting my breath.

In—one.

Out—one.

In—two.

Out—two.

It went well, or it did until I reached nine and then lost count, not able to remember if I was at nine or if I'd just counted nine or was reminding myself that nine was next. And so it went.

After a while (I'm not sure how long I sat there) I figured my first meditation period was a success—plus my feet were totally asleep—so I decided to take a break.

I went to work tidying up my camp, gathered more wood—caught myself a couple times talking to myself—had a bite to eat and decided I needed to have some exercise so I headed out on a hike to the truck stop, a good way down the highway.

Since I didn't have a watch, there really isn't any telling exactly how long it took to get there. All I'm sure about is the fact that my feet were sore and my head tired from all the thinking a good walk will inspire after a morning of introspection.

For whatever reason I'd gotten it into my head that I should call Sarah to let her know I was grateful for all she did for me. In a moment of weakness—or perhaps a moment of clarity (or boredom)—I used one of my last coins to call her.

"I'm so glad you called," she said from the other end. "I was so worried I'd never hear from you again. Look, I'm sorry I pried. Your business is yours, I understand. We all have a past..."

"Hey, it's not your fault—I'm the one who got all heavy with you. But none of that matters now all right? I'm working things out and understand where and what I've got to be—it's all going to be just fine." Despite the words rolling out of my mouth without effort, it was great to hear her voice.

I told her of my discovery in the woods—she didn't really say much but stressed that she wanted to see me.

"Come on. We can have a few drinks, I'll feed you and you can go back and be a monk or mountain man or Bigfoot—whatever. I just want to spend time with you, no strings attached."

After I hung up I thought to myself that morning meditation must do strange things to the brain—or else I'd been alone too long in the woods already. Sarah said she was going to borrow a friend's car and come pick me up. And I told her I thought that sounded like a great idea.

I poked around in the truck stop for a while, cleaning myself up like a teenybopper going out on a first date.

Looking at myself in the mirror of the men's room as truckers passed behind giving side glances on their way to the urinals, I mumbled about how I'd finally lost my mind. I think most of the burly, beer-bellied audience would have agreed.

But Sarah showed up, smiling from behind the wheel of a huge 1970's land yacht.

She smelled great. We kissed and before we'd even left the parking lot it was as if nothing had even happened.

She looked as good as she smelled and from the glances she was throwing my way and the way she was squeezing my hand and rubbing my thigh, she was really happy to see me.

On our way back to her place we made plans to go for a few drinks and then get a bite to eat or go for a walk.

But as it turned out, we dropped the car off at her place, ran to the door and before it had closed behind us were already all over each other.

There on the door mat we made love amid the pile of clothes we'd ripped off each other (once again). When we finished we just lay there, bodies dripping with sweat, arms and legs wrapped together.

I couldn't help but think to myself that this day had ended a lot differently than I'd intended it to.

# Back

Call it a feat of tremendous willpower—but while Sarah wanted me to stay over, after a good meal and loading me down with supplies, I talked her into taking me back to the truck stop. I saw the look on her face and knew she had to make an effort to not blurt out something about my not wanting her to see the cabin or something similar. But she only smiled and said she'd be happy to give me a lift back as long as I promised we'd get together again in a few days. I agreed.

After the ride back which seemed really quite short, we kissed goodbye. I laughed when she started filling my pockets with quarters—enough to call her regularly for a few months. Then I waved and headed back down the highway with my bags of food and other assorted things she decided I needed.

As her car pulled out into the road I looked toward her, shaking my head. She really was great. I felt sorry for her, obviously head over heels for me.

The walk back to the cabin wasn't too bad, but my fingers and arms were killing me from hauling the bags all the way. By the time I got back it was starting to get dark and I had to fumble around a bit to get my fire started so I'd be able to see for the next few hours.

Mildly aggravated with myself that I'd let almost a full day go by without much of my new found training, I decided to sit down, as the fire crackled to life, back straight, counting my breaths.

Thankfully this new attempt at meditation seemed to come a little easier, though I caught myself more than once drifting off into a fantasy about Sarah and various deviant sexcapades. Some kind of thoughts for a hermit reclusive aspiring Bodhisattva?!

Oh well, at least it was an attempt.

Afterwards, as I dozed off in the heat of the fire, munching on a bag of chips Sarah had given to me, I decided I'd have to go out into the surrounding area and do some exploring and see what there was to see.

# Views

I started the next morning back on my new routine of morning meditation and everything went remarkably well. I sat, counted breath and apart from a strange fascination in watching it play with dust particles in a beam of sunlight, the meditation period flowed perfectly.

After I was finished and tidied the place up a little I headed down the creek, deeper into the wilderness, away from my cabin and the roaring highway.

I stuck to the edge of the creek where the soil started to make way for the round rocks of the creekbed.

It was a beautiful day. The sky was blue and the sun felt great on my face.

From where the cabin was it was easy to forget there were amazing mountains sitting silently around me like ancient buddhas unmoving, waiting for those on a spiritual journey to be awed by their simple amazingness. The thick forest was not only hiding my cabin from the world, but the world from me.

Walking beside the creek was almost tranquillising. The gurgling sound the water made against the rocks was just loud enough to be the number one thing on the mind as I wandered nearby. It was like a gentle blanket, keeping out needless distraction. All that existed was the earth under my feet, the creek and me.

As I rounded a bend I saw a fang of rock jutting out of the trees and was instantly in love. "Wow," were the only words that could find their way out of my mouth—but they described everything perfectly.

I spent a few hours studying the mountain, laying out the best route to climb it.

Standing at its base looking up I thought about what it would be like to be on its side looking down, imagining that I could just slightly make out a blue tinge under the trees that must be my tarp roof.

As soon as I saw that massive monolith I knew we were going to have a date together. The feeling was so strong that I felt an odd deja vu, as if I'd already climbed it and was coming home again, seeing a familiar friend.

Picturing the route I would take up the mountain I literally had to drag myself away—climbing would have to wait for another day.

Truth was that I'd never tried to climb a whole mountain before and the thought scared me—but then again I'd never seen anything like this mountain before. It was perfection, a mountain from my dreams, everyone's dreams—it was the mountain. Every cell in my body was begging for me to give it a go. But I knew rock-climbing is one thing, and climbing up an entire mountain is another—but I was keen to learn more about that massive piece of rock—I realized I needed to recognize the difference between a climb and an expedition.

Nothing was going to stop me from making my way up there, touching heaven and earth, seeing in myself what I could only pretend to know.

Climbing that mountain scared me sure, but the thought of not heading up there frightened me even more. If I was launched on this whole voyage from a simple scamper up a slab of rock what would climbing an obviously sacred mountain do? I had no idea but I needed to find out.

Every cell in my body was calling out for me to put flesh to rock and do what I had to do to get up there. I knew already that there would be no turning back now, I was too far gone—this was my mountain.

Saluting the new friend I'd found I decided to turn back and head for home.

Wandering the way I'd come earlier in the day I couldn't get the thoughts of climbing out of my head. I felt like a little child excited about a plan to build a club house in a secret place or like a married man entertaining some erotic fantasy about the woman he'd just met.

I felt alive but fixated. It was as if seeing that mountain was what my whole life had been about.

After I'd rounded the same bend in the creek that I first noticed the mountain, I saw my second strange sight of the day. Actually, I thought I was hallucinating somehow when I saw them. But they were all very much real.

Sitting only a stone's throw from my cabin, near the edge of the creek were a handful of robed, shaven head monks.

I just stood there not quite sure what to do. While I'd read a lot about Buddhism, apart from that one glimpse in that temple, I'd never seen a real Buddhist monk. And never saw one outside of that isolated experience which I still wasn't sure what to make of. So for all intensive purposes I'd never seen an actual Buddhist monk in my life and I couldn't come up with a reason why I'd start seeing them now—especially out in the middle of nowhere.

I'm not sure how long I stood there, staring at them but in time, one of the group noticed me and motioned to the rest and the whole bunch of them turned and waved.

This was a very weird and interesting day.

# Them

"Hi," I said waving to them.

They waved back and although we were still quite a distance apart I could tell they were smiling.

Paying attention to the loose round rocks, I made my way over, wondering all the way, "what the hell are a bunch of monks doing beside my creek, near my cabin, out here?"

They were the kind of thoughts you hate thinking while they're coming out. But thoughts have a way of coming out whether you like them or not.

Looking up occasionally as I scrambled closer, I could see they were still smiling, watching me (likely wondering the same things about me that I was wondering about them).

"Hi," I said again, finally coming within talking distance.

"How are you," an older looking monk smiled at me from the same boulder that I'd sat on when I first found the creek.

I quickly scanned the group—six of them—all neatly shaved and robed in the sheet-like costumes of Buddhist monks.

"Are you Buddhist monks?" I asked already knowing the answer but hoping for a bridge into conversation. And at the same time, fear of a repeat of my last attempt at conversation with a Buddhist monk.

"Yes we are," the older one said placing his palms together, bowing slowly.

I bowed my head in return, a little uneasy but not wanting to show disrespect.

"We are of the Nipponzan Myohoji order—a Buddhist peace organization," he said bowing again. This time I bowed as closely as I could to the way he had.

"We are walking for peace across Canada—it is also our form of training."

"I see," I said biting the inside of my lip, still half expecting them to disappear at any time, being some strange result of a tough hike and lack of lunch.

But my lip hurt and they remained. I could taste blood in my mouth.

Slowly I scanned the group looking at them one by one.

"So, you are walking and meditating for peace?"

"A monk once thought about peace and Buddhism. The two should go very much hand in hand. He decided enough time was spent alone, meditating in temples away from the world. If Buddhist monks became a moving, mobile community spreading peace as they go, some great things may happen along the way."

I smiled realizing this old man was telling me exactly what I had been thinking lately, only I wasn't a monk.

"You're talking about spreading the dharma, moving it through the world, bringing the word of peace as you go. Like lighting a matching in a the darkness and then another and another, though a dark room—soon if enough matches are lit, the darkness will fall away."

The old monk smiled. "And if some matches go out, others will always be lighting up somewhere else in the room—we just have to get out there and make sure there are enough matches."

We looked into each other's eyes. This time we smiled the genuine smiles of two people who understand each other fully.

For the first time since I'd heard of Buddhism, and all the

things Jo had told me more recently about the Buddhist idea that all of the teachings of the Buddha were sent down all this time through direct transmission—one mind to another over more than two thousand years—it all made sense. I was witnessing for myself the teaching—or at least a portion of it. It felt very special, like wind blowing gently through wind chimes—I was getting part of it and it was beautiful. But I also knew there was a huge amount I still had no idea about, and the wind was nowhere near my chimes.

"I know you probably have a far way to go today, but I have a place in the woods here. I'm living here by the creek, away from everything. I guess I aspire to be a monk like all of you—but I think I do better on my own. Too much of people, and I start to lose touch with who I am."

The old monk just smiled.

I realized I was tripping over my words, obviously caused by my excitement at meeting such an interesting group and the fact that apart from conversations with myself I was somewhat missing talking to others. I may have been enjoying the life of a hermit but I'd never take a vow of silence.

"What I'm trying to say is, would you all like to come over to my cabin, I can make a fire, cook some dinner and if you want, you can camp out for the night—my woods are your woods."

They looked at each other, at the older monk and then back at me nodding and bowing.

Helping them to gather up the few bags they had, I led the way back to my cabin.

Turning back to watch them tug at their robes as they stepped up into the woods I giggled to myself at how strange life was. I find a wilderness retreat by chance, fashion myself into some sort of neo-Buddhist hermit and along come a group of monks to check on my progress—or if nothing else, to prod me another step along this path.

# Turning

I realized very quickly how the monks preferred silence to talking. They weren't rude when I broke the quiet to ask a question or make an observation but a look can tell more than a lecture sometimes.

I could remember something Jo had told me at some point that went something like, a rattling mouth usually means an undisciplined mind. It's probably true.

They were great guests, gathering wood for the fire, thanking me greatly for the meal (rice and carrots—both from Sarah) and one even decided to busy himself with fortifying my blue tarp. And he did a great job of it too.

"We were hoping you wouldn't mind us camping here with you tonight," the older monk said sitting down beside me in front of the crackling fire. "We don't want to be a burden on you but we walked quite far today and aren't expected in Calgary until late tomorrow."

I was nodding before my mouth even opened. "Oh, of course—I'm just sorry my cabin isn't large enough to fit everyone. But we have enough wood to keep the fire warm—we could all sleep out here and you could have the cabin if you wish," I said gesturing to my blue-roofed abode.

"Oh, no," he said shaking his head and clapping his hand on my knee. "I'm not so old that I don't enjoy a good sleep under the stars beside such a great and comfortable fire. Besides, sleeping and looking up at those ancient stars makes me feel young."

I grinned.

"But before we go to sleep we have our evening meditation—you are welcome to sit with us, if you wish."

Nodding I said, "I'd love to—I've been including meditation in my daily routine."

"Good then," he said getting up, motioning to the others that it was time for their training.

There are few things in life that you know will make a lasting impact on you. But as I sat there silently looking at the earth in the growing gloom with that small group of Buddhist peace monks I knew things were happening for a good reason—like they always do.

Sitting silently, the sound of the creek seemed to get louder and louder and out of nowhere, in the darkness I could swear I saw a swirling river running only a few feet from me into the shadows. A whirlpool spun slowly only an arm's length away and as I gazed at it, unmoving, I realized that while the whirlpool was a separate thing it was still very much part of the river. It was with this slow, calm logic that I started to see the whole of the universe in the same light, always flowing around into and through all things and while we think ourselves as separate from the rest of everything, we are really only a whirlpool in the vast river or the universe. And within us the entire universe flows, just as in that whirlpool the whole river exists—a small piece is still perfection of the whole.

I didn't say anything when we finished, keeping my small experience to myself. Instead, after the meditation was over we talked for a short while about their organization, about their quest for peace, my own questions about Buddhism and meditation and about the simple joy of sitting in the glow of a warm fire.

Soon the monks were pulling their bed rolls out and before I knew it we were all lying around the fire.

It was very easy to forget that this was a group of monks that I'd somehow bumped into in the middle of nowhere. I could remember my mother's words from years earlier when she heard I was going on a short trip by myself. "It is always interesting to travel alone, because you meet more people." Moms are always right about things.

As we drifted off to sleep I thought about the fact that while we had talked about many deep issues about life, never once did we talk about our own personal baggage. It had been as if our—or at least my—self had just dropped away. If only for a short while.

The monks were softly snoring under the ancient sky and I was starting to nod off myself, I looked over at the old monk that had treated me as well as the monks that walked with him all this time. I realized I didn't even know his name. But the best thing was that it didn't even matter.

# Walking

We meditated again in the morning but most of the time I sat I just kept wanting to look over at the monks to see what they were doing, how they looked—if they were still there.

Knowing that these individuals' job 24 hours a day was basically to be peace, calm and serenity was, to say the least, very cool. And these monks seemed to carry an air of that coolness with them—or maybe it was just me projecting that onto them, I'm not sure but it was great to be near them.

And so I sat, trying to watch my breath but mostly seeing them even if only in my mind.

Soon after, without much talking they started gathering their gear to get back on the road.

"I really wish I could join you on your walk but I think I have things that need to be done here. I think I've run far enough."

The old monk smiled and said nothing.

"You don't know how much of an honour it was to meet you—it really was something special for me," I said wanting to reach out and hug the calm old man.

He put his palms together bowing slightly. "And we have to thank you for the kindness you have shown to us. It was a very pleasant evening," he took my hand, shaking it. "Thank you very much."

He looked over at the others waiting patiently as ever.

"We really must be going. But I hope you continue your training and find what it is you are seeking here in the forest under your blue roof."

The old man who suddenly seemed as ancient as the stars he had talked about so lovingly the night before, bowed his head and turned, heading through the woods back towards the creek and the highway. The other monks fell in line behind him quietly.

For a few seconds I just stood there watching them head off through the trees. Then I decided to follow the odd moving sangha to the highway.

It was somewhat surprising how fast the old fellow moved. By the time I'd broken through the trees he was already being helped up to the highway by a younger monk who was pretty much pulling the old man up the loose gravel to the flat paved road.

I followed them up the bank and watched the monks silently walking in single file, moving with smooth silent precision—their eyes looking downward at every step they made.

It really was something to see—like a gentle snake rolling its way down the road.

Standing there watching them until they were only small points on the black asphalt I thought to myself how in another time, not too long ago, I would have begged to be part of their silent caravan.

But not now.

After last night's meditation I knew that all of us were just fine where we were, rotating in our own whirlpools and that the universe would work everything out in the end. I thought back to St. Joseph and the way that despite being put before the Inquisition for his levitating, flying, or whatever it was, he still remained calm and peaceful as if nothing in the world could matter. And he was right. I really felt like things were starting to come together the way they were intended to and it gave me a feeling of calm in the pit of my stomach—something that I couldn't remember feeling since maybe childhood.

I sat on the edge of the road like that, legs dangling over the embankment, enjoying the morning sun and a highway not yet roaring awake.

Looking towards the moving grey-white water and the forest behind it, it was easy to forget that I was sitting on the side of one of the busiest roads in North America, that is, it would have been easy to forget except for the transport trucks that occasionally zoomed past sending tiny bits of dirt into my mouth. Sitting there it was so easy to be caught up in the view and the big sky above me—life really was an amazing trip.

Gazing into the creek where it flowed under the highway I thought of the whirlpools and how they and the whole river are always changing, always moving. Who could say what any of us would be the next moment in time? Our own rivers and whirlpools are always swirling us around, bumping us into this part of the river and then that and while they seem so different, so out of place, everything is still perfect, unsymmetrical symmetry.

I looked back down the highway at the little specks of monk in the distance, whirlpools flowing down their own river but still very much part of mine.

A small cloud floated in front of the sun taking the warmth from my face for a moment, but I knew it would be back.

The darkness was lifting.

# Curse

God only knows how long I sat there since I didn't have a watch on, and I was far too content with myself grooving on the inner workings of the universe and feeling a little too much pride in myself for the insights. But while I was busy patting myself on the back I didn't notice the police cruiser—that is, I didn't see it until it was already too late to slink back down to the creek and into the woods.

No lights were flashed, no sirens sounded—but when I looked over my shoulder and saw the car pull over and stop a few feet from me, I felt as if I'd just been nabbed in a high speed chase.

I didn't even get up or try to leave. I knew full well that it was far too late for any of that, the river was flowing and I'd just have to go with it.

As the officer cracked open the door of his patrol car and hauled himself out, sliding his baton into its holder on his belt, I looked back towards where the monks would have been if they were still visible, part of me wishing I'd gone for a walk with them.

"Hello there," the officer said adjusting his gun belt, resting one hand on top of the revolver, the other on his hip. I had the sudden feeling I was about to be dealing with a cop who had never drawn his gun but had always dreamed of using it, especially if no one would ever have to know. His thumb rubbed the metal of the weapon.

"Hi," I said back squinting up at him, grit from the dust he'd made pulling over getting into my eyes and mouth. I could feel it crunching in my teeth as my jaw tensed, waiting for whatever was to happen next.

"What are you up to today?"

"Just sitting sir," I said truthfully but knowing it wasn't the kind of answer he was looking for.

"I can see that—do you realize how dangerous it could be sitting on the side of the highway?"

I looked past his cruiser and then back over my other shoulder. "I don't think the busy part of the day has come yet—it's pretty early."

He pushed down on his gun, shifting his weight. The leather of his belt and holster creaked.

"It only takes one vehicle. So what are you doing sitting out here? Looking for a ride or something?"

Looking back towards where my cabin hid in the woods, just wanting to reassure myself that it was safe from sight I slowly tilted my head back, looking up at him. "Have I done anything wrong?"

"I don't know, have you?"

I was getting the idea this cop was just looking for something or someone to turn a boring morning on patrol into something a little more exciting.

"Why don't you get up and come over to the car and we can talk." It wasn't a question but a command.

"No offence but we are talking sir."

"Just get up and come to the car, we don't need this to be a hassle."

"I was just sitting here...I don't want trouble...but I haven't done anything."

He glared at me.

"Look, we can do this nice and friendly or we can stop being friendly—it's up to you. I just want to ask you a few questions that's all—personally I don't want to stand out here and get hit by a truck."

At first I thought about protesting more but I knew we both had no doubt in our minds that either I was going to get up or he was going to force me to.

I stood up slowly and walked to the passenger side of the car. He followed at a safe distance, two or three steps behind me, hand still on his firearm.

When we got beside the cruiser he tapped my elbow asking, "can I see some identification please?"

Reaching into my pockets I started emptying them onto the hood of his car unsure exactly where my identification could be in the deep recesses of my coat. He wasn't taking his eyes off of me for a minute, his hand still fingering the butt of his gun. I couldn't help but think to myself that with no witnesses around he could get rid of a vagrant like me in a heart beat if he was so inclined.

Used tissue, a penny or two, paper, a lighter—everything came out in handful after handful. It was actually kind of amazing to see all of the things you forget about buried in the bottom of a pocket.

He pushed through the pile with a pen he'd pulled from his chest pocket.

Fishing out my identification from the pile he continued to push his way through the pile until the pen stopped. My heart dropped into my shoes.

Somehow I'd totally forgotten about the joint Dwight and Logan had given to me when I jumped out of their van in almost exactly the same place as I was now standing.

Slowly his eyes raised up from his unmoving hand—I knew he was already staring at me before our eyes met.

"It looks like we have ourselves a little trouble here."

Looking at the identification in his hand I said, "more trouble than you know about."

I slowly opened the door of the cruiser and sat down inside without saying another word.

In a very orderly manner he picked everything up off the hood of his car and put the joint into his pocket along with my identification.

Once in the car he entered information into a small computer that was built into the vehicle, looked at me and said simply, "hmm."

A quick u-turn and we were headed back towards Banff.

Apart from a few sideways glances, nothing was said or done for the remainder of our trip except for periodic movements of the wheel. It was very weird—the kind of feeling you'd get from your father when he was really pissed off— "don't even talk to me."

I guess it was at least partially to make me feel guilty. It wasn't working—but I did feel stupid and caught myself a few times fantasizing about making a run for it when the car stopped.

I won't go into all the mundane details of being dragged into the police station—everyone has seen it in countless television shows and movies. Suffice it to say, I was processed. I wasn't thrilled.

I had no plan to be overly helpful, but it didn't take him long to figure out who I was and the fact I was listed as a missing person.

"There have been a lot of people wondering what happened to you," the officer said from across his desk. I wondered to myself if the joint was still in his pocket.

"Really?" What else could I say?

"Yeah—do you want to tell me what you've been running from?"

"Not really. I mean, does it really matter? I'm not missing now and I think I have a right to live my life the way I want to—I mean I haven't hurt anyone. I've just been running."

He looked at me blankly. After a moment or two he opened a file he'd brought over to his desk and read from a sheet of paper that had my picture on it—obviously the missing person poster I'd seen before or one similar.

I almost felt like taking it off of him, some strange part of me wanting to take another look at the document—it's not every day you see yourself in a wanted poster.

"You have a wife and yet for over a year and a half you couldn't even pick up the phone to let her know you were still alive?"

I jumped like a door had slammed shut behind me.

"A year and a half—it can't have been that long," I said moving closer to the desk. "There must be a mistake there."

"No mistake. It's all right here. I don't know what you've been up to or where you've been but I think you need to make a phone call."

I didn't know what to say, and don't think I really heard what he was saying, just looking at the black and white photocopy of myself looking back at me, smiling upside down from across the desk. I could remember the day Mary had snapped that shot of me with the camera I'd given to her as a birthday present.

"A year and a half." It literally felt like the room was spinning.

The officer closed the folder and moved his phone towards me.

"Look I'm just going to let this joint disappear. All I could really do is slap you on the wrist but in exchange I want you to pick up the phone and let your family know you are alive. I can't force you to and I can't force you to go home but I strongly suggest you let people know you aren't dead—at least give them that."

His words seemed to be crawling out of his mouth, his lips barely moving.

I just sat still, looking at him and the phone.

"I don't think I remember the phone number." My voice seemed to be coming from somewhere in the distance.

He reached across the desk and pulled the phone closer to him, picked up the handset, opened the folder and started pressing numbers.

I could hear the number he'd just dialled starting to ring on the other end.

Taking the phone from his ear, he handed it back to me.

It was still ringing.

The phone looked huge.

Watching a hand reach out for it, it took a second or two to register that it was my own hand.

As I brought the receiver to my ear I heard the ringing stop with a click.

"Hello?"

It was Mary's voice.

# Echo

"Hello," she said again.
"Hi Mary, it's me."
Silence.

I looked over at the cop—he was going to shoot me if I didn't go through with this.

"Mary it's me."

"Oh my God," her voice was trembling as she spoke. "You're all right? I mean...I thought..." she was starting to cry.

"Mary, I'm okay, I just wanted you to know I'm all right."

"Where are you...where have you been?" she said with a voice nearly stuttering with emotion.

"I know I hurt you and I'm sorry about that, but..." the tears came from nowhere. I covered my eyes with my free hand, lowering my head feeling overly conscious of the police officer watching from across the desk.

"I don't know what I'm doing but I've got to do it." I managed to get out between shuddering sobs. My tongue felt two sizes too big.

"What do you mean? You've been gone so long, what am I supposed to do?"

I didn't know what to say, listening to her crying on her end and wiping tears from my face on my own. We just sat there crying on the phone for what seemed like hours. And as usually happens in emotional situations, listening to crying only makes you cry more. I wanted to hang up the phone, or get up and run—I wanted to be just about anywhere else other than right there, right now.

"I'm not coming home," I finally forced out of my mouth almost surprised to hear the words myself.

"But...why? What have I done? Why are you doing this?"

No answer was going to be adequate. "I don't know. I have no real idea why I'm doing anything that I've been doing but it doesn't have anything to do with you personally. You're great—I just can't be there."

"Don't you love me? This is all my fault isn't it? I know I've been too pushy all this time, pressuring you to get a better job and wanting to have kids and expecting so much from everything. I'm sorry."

A part of me wanted to tell her anything that would make this moment and all similar ones just vanish but truth was she was right, it was her fault and everyone else's fault as well. The whole damn world was to blame for the bullshit that had been clearing from my eyes. I wanted to tell her that her only salvation was not to find Jesus or anything else but instead to tell everything else to go fuck itself—nothing matters—when it comes down to it, each and every single one of us is nothing more than a freshly dug grave. That what does matter is breathing, seeing sun make a blue tarp seem to glow in the morning, the smile of a shaven-headed lesbian samurai after she'd just helped you kick heroin, climbing a mountain, stretching out in the warmth of a summer day. What doesn't matter is pretty much everything else my life had been before. But instead I told her something much more simple and infinitely cruel.

"It isn't you. It's just...I love you too much. Every time I look at you, think of you...it tears me apart. I'd kill myself but I'm afraid that in doing that I'd be forced to spend an eternity looking at you, thinking over what I'd done."

I looked up at the cop. He just sat there, leaning back, arms crossed over his chest looking as unemotional as he did when he first picked me up.

I bent back over and put my hand over my face again.

"What did I ever do? You told me we'd get through all of this. That everything was going to be all right." She was whimpering. But she was right, for months before I left she would ask me what was wrong, begged me to talk to her and I'd always just smiled and told her everything would be fine.

"I know I did but one day everything just changed and I couldn't put up with the bullshit. I couldn't go back to work and contribute to an RRSP, floss my teeth, comb my hair and say 'yes please' and all that crap. I saw with a clarity that I've never known that life as we live it is just fantasy—and I don't want any more of it. Truth is, if you want me to be honest, I'm glad things worked out the way they did for us. Without you I don't think I would have ever found the true level of suffering there is in this life. If there is a hell Mary, it can't be much worse than living in this reality we've cooked up for ourselves, going along with it even though we know better deep down, that life isn't supposed to be the way it is."

She was silent.

"I'm sorry I hurt you but you'll be better without having me there to add to your life. Those Buddhists are right, life is suffering and believe it or not but my not being there is making yours less."

"What kind of shit is that?"

"What do you mean," I asked?

"Are you in some sort of cult or what? What is going on with you? What did I do to deserve this?"

"What did you do? What did I do to deserve the shit you've put me through. If you only listened to me, listened to one thing I said to you things could have been different. Truth is I don't think I ever loved you—I was railroaded into marrying you because I was to much of a coward to say no..." I stopped myself short. I couldn't believe the words that were coming out of my lips. But the truth was that I believed every thought that I was trying my hardest to hold back, that in the end it was her fault that the house and life we worked so hard to get perfect was empty.

Mary screamed into the phone. "You're a real bastard you know—I really wish I'd never met you." There was venom in her words, even with the distance between us I could feel it.

I didn't say a word.

"Why the fuck did you even call? Did you just want to fuck with my mind—open up wounds that were almost healed?"

"The police asked me to call."

"The pol...well you can go fuck yourself. And do both of us a favour and never call again or show yourself around here...or best yet, go ahead and kill yourself and get it over with, the rest of the world has begun to forget you anyway. As far as I'm concerned, you died a long time ago."

"Mary, I..." but I realized the line was dead. She had slammed the phone down.

I just sat there listening to the sound of the dead line.

Part of me wanted to call her back and beg forgiveness, the other half was glad it was all over and I didn't have to lurk behind the shadows any longer.

Slowly the phone slid from my ear. I looked up not really focusing on anything almost wanting to ask the officer what had just happened. But I knew full well. And although reality was feeling totally screwed up and twisted around I felt sure everything was going to be all right. I felt like a weight had been lifted.

A book had closed. I could feel it, that strange certain feeling you have when you read the last lonely pages of a novel and begin to understand how everything was going to work out, one way or another.

I always hated those end pages in books. It didn't matter if it was an epic novel or a cheap comic book. Those pages always left me thinking there had to be more or that the writer would pen another story that continued exactly where the one in my hand had left off. But things rarely work out that way.

Sitting, staring at the telephone handset, listening to the sound of a dead line coming from somewhere far off in the distance I knew there was no more to this story. Sure, another book was about to open for me but this story, this life I'd known for so long was at an end.

Watching my hand place the phone back together in its cradle I could feel the cathartic finality of the situation fully.

"I guess that is that," the cop said, eyes still on me as ever.

I felt like telling him to go fuck himself, but instead mumbled, "I guess you're right."

"I'm good to my word, I'm going to let you go now that things have been taken care of. And if what I overheard is right you won't be heading back home."

"No, no I don't think that is going to happen—not that I want it to."

"So now we have another little problem."

I didn't want to hear any more of his little insights. While I felt lighter, I also felt like someone had just taken a round out of me. I wanted to lie down.

"You see, I can't just drop you off at the side of the road and I don't really want to see you hanging out around town with nowhere to go."

Looking down at my shoes I said quietly, "I have a friend I've been staying with. I could call her, have her pick me up and I would be out of your hair. I know I could stay with her and I wouldn't be a bum or anything on your streets." It was a kind of half truth but it was enough.

He nodded his head and pushed the phone towards me again.

# Baby steps

After a lecture on the dangers of being a drugged-out fuck up, the big cop showed me to the front waiting area where I told Sarah I'd meet her—thankfully she was home when I called.

The second the door opened and she entered the detachment I knew she wasn't thrilled to be picking someone, anyone up at the police station, that much was obvious from the look she darted at me. Before the door had even closed behind her I was up and escorting her back out the door.

"Remember what I told you," the officer said from behind the bullet-proof glass window over the counter. He smiled mechanically at Sarah and looked back at me. "Keep your nose clean. If we need you to answer any questions or tie up any loose ends I've got your friend's number—you will be available through this number right?"

"He'll be with me," Sarah spoke up.

He nodded, shot another look my way and walked away.

Sarah and I barely said two words that whole day. She could tell I was in no mood to discuss anything in depth and I knew she was pissed off about having to pick me up at the police station. I gave her the basic facts about how I'd been picked up for sitting on the side of the highway, discovered with a joint, found to be a missing person and forced to call the place I used to think of as home.

It wasn't a hero's welcome after being out on a mystical quest but it was a homecoming of sorts.

On the plus side, apart from the joint, I'd broken no law—I was just a deadbeat husband.

At one point I started talking—more like babbling—about St. Joseph and the Inquisition but only started crying and headed for the bedroom. Sarah just let me go.

Nothing looked the same. Even the sunlight showing through the window of her livingroom seemed to make the dust dance in a strange, unreal manner. Everything was all akimbo. My head was spinning but at the same time I felt new. Lying across the bed quietly crying I thought to myself that this must be the way newborn babies feel, happy to be experiencing a new world but totally overpowered by emotion.

For hours I just lay like a corpse on Sarah's bed, eyes closed. I could hear her occasionally making odd noises from the other rooms of her place. I knew she likely wanted to say something but simply couldn't find adequate words.

I wish I could say that all those hours I spent reading the back of my eyelids, I was busy dreaming up grandiose plans of how to continue my adventure, the next step in my personal evolution, but in reality I just stretched myself out and stared at the coloured patterns in the void behind of my closed eyes.

Doors opened, closed, things were moved, Sarah walked around and made other noises I couldn't quite figure out—and I didn't really have any interest in. It was all like some strange out of body experience.

Occasionally she would pop her head into the room. I could see her face creep in through the crack in the door and then silently disappear. She just looked in on me and then left.

But with darkness eventually starting to make its way in, my eyes shot open as she whispered at one point, "are you just going to stay in that one spot forever?"

Slowly I sat up.

"I've just been thinking."

"About what," she asked?

"I don't really know...things I guess."

"Like..." she waited, her head still just hanging suspended in the open space between the door and its frame.

"I don't know, just about what I'm going to do now."

"And what have you decided?"

I got up and walked to the door, opening it and pulling her towards me.

"I've decided I feel happy where I am right now. For the first time I can honestly say I'm being the real me and living what I'd consider a real life. And I can't think of anyone else I'd rather be standing, holding right at this moment."

She put her head on my shoulder. "That is one very good answer."

"Thanks. And thank you for being here for me. You really are great."

She pulled back and looked into my eyes in the dim light. "I really am a sucker—I must either be nuts or totally crazy about you."

That was one of those things where you're better off not saying anything after someone says it to you. We just stood there holding each other.

I didn't feel like a million bucks but life didn't feel all that bad either.

It was the first time in years that I could honestly say I didn't have to do something or go somewhere—I wasn't running. And it was a very strange feeling.

Thinking back to another life when I was younger, training

to run 10 km races. Halfway through the circuit my body felt like the run would never end—mind and body playing tricks, trying to get those legs to stop. But when it was over and the finish line was far behind there was always a strange feeling of, "OK...now what..." Now it felt the same—like there should be bells, or fireworks, or anger, but instead there was only a very still inner silence and a subtle secret knowing.

I was a new man. And it felt both good and frightening.

As I pulled Sarah closely to me, she rubbed my back slowly, lovingly like a mother would to a small child. I felt very lucky.

"Sarah," I whispered to her.

"Hmm?"

"Endings have a strange silence to them."

# Light

My eyes opened. Waking in the morning perfectly and peacefully, I couldn't help but wish I could start every day the same way.

The faint echo of my dreams still lingered on the fringes, images of that perfect mountain a short hike from my cabin—it left me with that familiar, throbbing desire to reach its peak. From the dream I could still remember floating like an angel over the rocky terrain, looking down at the most perfect route. I soared up the face and when I was only a short throw from the top I opened my eyes and woke up.

Without a jolt or anything else—which had become my regular way to wake up—I simply breathed in the familiar smells of another day—I didn't even feel like I'd just woken up. Actually it felt like I'd slept so well the cells and DNA had created a whole new body, one that felt great.

I watched a ray of sunlight playing gently with the dust in the air, wondering to myself how I could ever have just walked past similar sights before, not seeing the perfection in the moment.

Rolling over to look at Sarah I realized one more part of the dream that had nearly evaporated as dreams do: I wasn't just flying up the mountain, I was gliding effortlessly, with smooth precision—but backwards like St. Joseph would have done. I could remember feeling a close, spiritual connection between the mountain, the sun and my own body floating with a fluid grace backwards in the air.

Sarah was sleeping silently beside me. Her hair glowed gold in the sunlight. She looked perfect sleeping there.

Strand by strand I gently brushed stray hair from her face. She was beautiful.

Thoughts of yesterday surfaced, images of Mary, Ginger, Jo, shooting up, stealing from that poor student, Mel, getting busted—I just let them go, truth was I knew all these images were phantoms of a past now long gone, I'd walked through a new door. What was done and gone was history—now is all that matters. I knew this or at least was darn good at talking myself into believing it.

As if she knew I was looking at her, Sarah slowly opened her eyes and smiled. We just lay there together, inches apart.

"I was thinking," I said.

"I thought I could smell something burning," she smiled.

"No, seriously—I'd like to take you to my place. My cabin in the woods that is, we can stay there together. It's a great place and I'm sure you'll love it. And then I was thinking there is a mountain pretty close by—a real beauty—I thought maybe we could try our hand at some mountaineering together. I've scrambled around it a bit and I'm pretty sure it would be a fun hike up, nothing too deadly."

She smiled at me—I already knew what her answer was going to be.

"That sounds great. I'd love to see your cabin and you know how much I love to climb," she said sitting up. The sheets dropped down as she did, exposing a breast. Gingerly and with a sly grin she pulled the covers up to her chin. I smiled.

"I don't know how much technical climbing there'll be, I

think most of it is just steep hiking. There might be a route or two we'll have to use gear with though."

"I've got a rope and packs and pretty much everything else...when do we leave?" she asked with wide eyes, looking deeply into mine.

"First I'm going to kiss you," I said reaching out to pull her closer. "Then we can get ready and head off. If that sounds good to you."

"It sounds pretty damn fine to me."

We slunk back down into the bed kissing amid the light show of beams of sparkling morning sunlight.

I was a great day to be alive.

# Out

It didn't take us too long to get our acts together and gather what we needed for our little trip.

Sarah actually did most of the packing while I showered and tried my best to stick to my pledge of morning meditation—but I was just too excited about getting back to the cabin and climbing that mountain that had literally haunted my dreams.

Always the trooper, Sarah made a quick call to a girlfriend who agreed to give us a ride out to the creek with the packs that Sarah had loaded up before I even realized it.

We didn't talk a word the whole ride there, just looked at each other with big toothy grins.

A couple of times I caught myself thinking back to the events of the day before and all the little details that had culminated with the impact of a small explosion. But I managed to put the images out of my mind—denial gets better with practise.

The thin layer of snow that had fallen seemed to amplify sounds as we got out of the car in about the same place I'd been dropped off and picked up from before.

It was great to see snow on the ground. And while it made the rocks around the creek a little slippery, snow added to the beauty of the spot.

We waved back at our ride who'd done a quick u-turn and was stopped, honking her horn and waving.

Taking Sarah's hand I led her over the old creekbed into the woods and on to my cabin.

With the blanket of snow it seemed like I'd been away forever, like a soft dust had fallen over everything.

"This is great," Sarah said grinning as we passed the last of the bushes and trees into the clearing. It was a great sight to see that blue tarped hut.

Looking over to her, gripping her hand a little tighter I asked, "are you serious—you really like it?"

"Oh yeah, it's great. Could use a woman's touch but it is as fantastic as you'd described it."

I looked at my simple home, remembering the monks and my joy in happening upon the remains of the cabin, and the work I did to rebuild it.

"Yeah, it is great isn't it? But by a woman's touch you just mean having you here right?"

She laughed and poked me in the ribs. "Don't worry, I won't mess with your stuff or try to plant a flower garden or anything."

Looking around I said, "actually a flower garden might not be a bad idea—except for the fact that with winter coming, for the next few months you'd have to do something about the ground freezing up, and of course the snow."

Waving her hand in the air Sarah walked towards the cabin, "details, details."

Once inside Sarah stood and looked around 360 degrees in the blue filtered light. "I could really take a liking to this place." We took our packs off and put them in the corner.

"So what now Grizzly?"

"Grizzly—I like the sound of that. Well, I guess the first thing I need to do is start up a fire—why don't you have a look around and I'll get things all toasty for us."

She nodded, reaching up to kiss my cheek. "That sounds like

a great idea."

We had a terrific night together, huddled in front of the fire, just enjoying each other's company. Amid the crackling of the flames we made plans to wake early in the morning and head for the mountain and our climb.

It was a beautiful night. The moon was half full and there were more stars in the sky than I could remember having seen in a long time.

Our eyes were starting to close on their own when we decided to turn in for the night. Sarah busied herself hanging a blanket she'd brought in the doorway to keep out the cold, while I sat tending to the last embers of our dying fire.

"Tell me something," she said from inside the cabin.

"Like what?"

"Yesterday you were so upset and today you haven't said a thing about what happened. Are you sure you're all right? I mean, we don't have to climb if you're not up to it."

While she was talking I was leaning way back looking up at the sky wondering to myself how many years had gone by since that same light I was looking at originally left the distant suns. Man was likely still huddling in caves afraid of the creatures prowling in the darkness.

Glancing back towards the cabin, I could barely make out Sarah's shadowy silhouette in the doorway.

"I don't know. I was messed up yesterday, I felt like the world had fallen all around me. But for some reason when I woke up this morning none of that seemed to matter. I had you, this cabin, and the thought of climbing that mountain."

Her dark figure didn't move.

Poking the fire with a stick the glowing remains of a log cracked apart. Bright sparks floated into the air for a few seconds.

"If you need to talk about things you do know I'm always

here for you."

I poked the embers again sending another swirling cloud of sparks into the air.

"I know."

Sarah disappeared from the doorway, I could hear her zipping the sleeping bags, getting our bed ready.

I poured a pot of water over the coals noticing how in the dark silence of the woods every sound seemed amplified, senses heightened. Or was it that without the distraction of actually seeing, things were just put into their own perspective.

The water made the coals pop and sizzle and steam rose up into the air. I mumbled to myself, "reality is actually clear and loud...everything else just drowns it out."

Putting the pot down I smiled, shrugged my shoulders and headed for the warm welcoming distraction from reality that I called Sarah—and it was all right.

# Steps

It wasn't morning yet when I jolted awake sitting upright, heart racing, body sweating.

Sitting there watching my breath in the cold morning air I could still feel the faint but close enough memories of a dream. I could remember faces and fire but not much else, that is except for a huge, looming presence hovering over me, crushing down on me like the weight of a thousand moons.

I woke with the feeling of a strange vertigo in my legs and the taste of bile in my mouth. And even though I was now wide awake, watching the smoke-like movement of my breath in the dim, cold blue, I could still feel the overwhelming feeling of the presence.

Looking over at Sarah sleeping warmly beside me, I watched her slowly breathing, eyes moving under her closed eyelids—she was going to be asleep for a while and I was wide awake. Knowing the kind of day we had ahead of us, trekking up the tooth of stone I couldn't help but wish I was still asleep too.

Instead of making a vain attempt at re-entering unconsciousness I opted to slowly slink my way out of the sleeping bags and blankets Sarah had fashioned into a snug bed the night before.

As quietly as possible I pulled my clothes on and crept outside.

The sky was a dull blue—but nowhere near as beautiful blue as my tarp—with the sun not quite up for the day yet. I looked up hoping to see the spectacular sky from the night before but apart from a stray star or two there wasn't much to be seen.

I headed for my favourite fir tree to keep up with my morning meditation. The massive tree was dry and clear all around its trunk and a soft bed of leaves and assorted other dry matter made for a great place to sit, contemplating the universe.

Sitting there slowly seeing my breath become more and more visible in the early light my thoughts drifted to Mary.

"You've done the best thing you could," the voice of my consciousness whispered lovingly from the darkness. "Attachment just leads to suffering—by leaving, nobody needs to attach to you and you don't need to dwell on life and death either."

These thoughts too I tried in vain to shake from my head.

I could remember Jo telling me at some point that trying to knock thoughts out of your head is like trying to walk calmly over broken glass barefoot—just can't happen, you just get better dealing with the reality of the situation.

Finally giving up, I shook my foot that had fallen asleep.

The sun was now more up than not. I stretched and rubbed my head.

"You enlightened yet?" a voice said from behind me.

Sarah was poking her head out from behind the blanket door—which had really done a great job through the night.

Smiling I turned towards her. "I don't know about enlightened but I do know that my mind likes to run all over the place. I'm haunted by memory and thoughts of the future, feelings, and just about everything else you could imagine."

"Well, I know a good cure for that—trying not to kill yourself while climbing up a mountain that really couldn't care less."

I stood up a little wobbly—I must have been sitting for some time but I wasn't at all sure how long.

We tidied up, repacked our things, had a bite and headed for the rock—actually we did everything near light speed, both wanting to start the climb.

There was still a light snow on the ground as I lead the way to the creek and on towards the mountain.

Sarah was a regular billygoat, leaping over logs, up one side of a boulder and down the other—smiling all the way. Most of the time I just stood back and watched her.

"The extra work is warming me up for the tough stuff ahead—you should try," she said while bouldering up another rock.

Shaking my head I said something about not being a morning person and just contented myself to stand and watch. As I've said before, there is something erotic about watching a woman climb. Determination, grace and power combine into one focused effort—and of course the tight climbing pants don't hurt either.

Needless to say, I just kept watching.

It really was a beautiful day to climb. The sky was bright and the sun shining. And while it was a little on the cool side—which gave me a slight tinge of apprehension since I knew full well it wasn't going to get warmer as we climbed higher—at least it would keep us cool as we worked our way up.

Standing looking up at the massive monolith I kicked myself for not finding out the name of the mountain. Sarah said she had no idea either and agreed that we should find out when we went back to town.

"But personally, I think we should call it Mount Sarah," she grinned.

"Oh, all right, that's not too egotistical."

"Don't be sad, there'll be other mountains we can name after you."

"Thanks, but to be honest I'd rather just be the nameless guy who climbed your mountain."

She stood there looking at me and then started howling with laughter.

"What's so funny?"

"That just sounded very...weird..."she giggled.

"Whatever. All I know is I'd rather not have a mountain named after me, sounds like bad luck—I mean most mountains are named after dead guys."

"Superstitious too," she was still laughing.

I glanced past her and headed for a goat path I'd found before that lead up a steep but hikeable slope.

Sarah grabbed my arm. "You know there are a lot of climbers who think you should ask permission from the mountain before you climb it."

Looking at her and then upwards, following the nearest edge of the crag to what I could see of the top. Almost like vertigo but different, a wave of foreboding swept over me. I took a few steps back, gazing intently at the ground to focus.

"Are you all right?"

"Yeah, I guess I just looked up too fast or something. I guess I'm just excited," I brushed the feelings off.

But I could remember the same feeling from my dream that shook me awake only a few hours earlier.

"So, what do you think?"

"About what?" I said brought back to the moment.

"Should we have some sort of ceremony?"

Realizing she had actually been serious I looked at her soberly, "oh, yeah sure. I think that would be a great idea. All the help we can get I guess."

But as we stood there in the shadow of the mountain it was obvious neither of us had any idea what we should do and in the end we each made a small cairn of rocks at the start of the trail and a couple silent prayers completed the job.

With the sun warming the rocks above us, we headed up.

# Altitude

I was right. The day was perfect and the climb amazing.

While every step took us higher and happier as we knew we were getting closer to the top, it was easy to forget that one wrong step and you'd be learning all new meanings for the word pain. But for the most part the climb was nothing more than a steep hike—very steep at times with a few scrambles upwards on hands and knees, but the trek was so far more fun than fight.

And we were making great time. So great in fact that when we reached an alpine meadow a few hours into the climb we decided to sit back and stop for a lunch break even though noon was at least an hour off.

By now the sun was well up and felt warm with our hearts beating strongly in our chests.

"It's really cool."

"What's that?" Sarah said looking up from the trail bar she was munching on.

I motioned around us. "All of this. From below it looks like the mountain is all just rock with a few trees clinging to the sides. But here we are having a picnic beside a mountain creek—it's a whole different world from a different perspective."

Sarah looked up at the bony finger of rock towering above us. It looked ominous, like some small child's version of what a mountain peak should look like.

"Yeah, it really makes you wonder what we'll find up there. I guess it's all like you say, perspective and about getting to the vantage point to see a certain thing from a different viewpoint."

"It's too bad we couldn't always see things in their totality—what it all means, what it's all like. But instead all we ever notice are the little things—snapshots in time."

Both of us looked off over the valley below. I couldn't get out of my mind the idea that everything is radically different from another point of view—I mean, it was something I knew already and had realized like a crack of thunder the day before I left for good but the truth is I never stopped to think that even that perspective could be seen so differently from another viewpoint. Actions could be both right and wrong all depending on the height that you're viewing them from. Suddenly the image of the oroboros, the ancient symbol of the snake eating its own tail came into my mind, almost as if it was hovering in the air in front of me.

"Yeah, I get it," I blurted out. Sarah looked over at me obviously jolted out of her meditation on the valley far below.

"You get...what?"

"The snake eating its tail...it's futile. All of us are eating our tails to save ourselves."

She leaned back as if she had to get a better view of me.

"There is an ancient symbol that for whatever reason just popped into my mind when we were talking a couple seconds ago. To be honest I can't really remember where I first heard of it but the thing I figured out is that life itself may not be futile, it is just that we put so much meaning on our actions and classify them all as either good or bad but the truth is that all are the same, or maybe all are dependent on the others. Without good there would be no bad. Without people lost there would be no-one found. Without suffering there would be no enlightenment.

Without a mountain there would be no reason to climb."

"Well, that much is obvious…is this high altitude getting to you?"

I smiled, nodding. "It might be. Lately I've been having these insights. I had one the other day. Things are really starting to fall into place for me. I'm starting to see my life and everyone's life as something far greater. And most importantly, I'm starting to see how everything is linked together. Without having met you I'd never have found the cabin or this mountain or whatever should come next. Everything is following, flowing the way it does, in a writhing, ever-turning wheel like the Buddhists call it or like a snake trying to catch its tail."

"Or it could just be the early signs of high altitude on the brain," Sarah said smiling as she gave me a shot in the arm.

I decided to just leave my little kensho where it fell and pick up my eating where it left off.

After we were done with the grub we didn't waste much time in heading up, nearly running up some parts.

Climbing can be a deceptive thing. You look up at the top—or what you think is the top and while you could swear you're continuing upwards, the distance to the top never seems to change. We began to realize this quickly only about an hour after our lunch snack in the meadow.

Things were really starting to get much steeper and soon we were pulling out our harnesses we'd brought with us and strapped on the rope and before we knew it we were using all of our skill and gear making our way up the face. Real climbing as I could hear disembodied voices calling from around me— "now you aren't hiking."

I started to wonder what I had gotten myself into.

While Sarah had done her share of mountaineering before, this was my first full mountain—and it was starting to scare me stiff. I was already higher up than I'd ever been and couldn't stop myself from looking down—way down into the valley.

On one pitch Sarah was lead climbing, I made the mistake of not just looking down but staring downwards, taking in all I could see, trying to focus on some tiny speck far below and make out what it was. All I learned was that it was a very long way down—further down than down had ever been.

Noticing the belay had stiffened up Sarah yelled down at me, "what's wrong...you all right?"

My legs were shaking and the rope that secured me to the rock face suddenly felt as thin as a strand of hair. But somehow I managed to break free from the downward spiral my vision was making and looked up at my climbing partner. "I'm fine," I lied to Sarah. "I just thought I saw something."

"Oh...well if you don't mind, I'd like it if you kept your eyes on me—if I fall I plan on landing right on your head."

I didn't say another word and I didn't dare fix my eyes on anything below us. And I couldn't tell Sarah I was scared out of my wits.

I may have been getting visions of enlightenment on the side of a mountain like some crazy Zen sage but I was starting to decide that mountains and me didn't necessarily agree.

The rest of the day was much of the same type of hard climbing as we had been struggling with since after lunch. While I was depending on her skill, stamina and ability I could see from the looks on her face that Sarah was getting frustrated too.

"A lot tougher climb than we thought it would be eh?" she said almost pleading for support.

"Yeah, I'm sorry—I thought it would be a simple climb up and climb down like it was this morning. Guess we're at the point now where we either climb down now and end up doing a lot of the down climbing in the dark or we stay up here for the night."

She nodded but didn't say a word, brushing grit off her knee.

"I think we should head back down to where we had lunch. It's quite a bit lower—it'll still be cold but not like up here."

She looked out over the open air towards the other peaks surrounding us—another view you can't really appreciate from lower vantage points. It was hard to believe there were people, cities and endless dreamed up problems down there. From up here all that seemed to exist on the Earth was mountain after mountain.

"Tomorrow we can get up early and make a hit at the top or climb back down—we just need to find a place to sleep safely, we can't sleep here."

I looked around at the small cliff-like outcropping we were huddled on top of. With our backs to the rock and our knees pulled to our chests there was just enough room for us to sit. Our packs were hanging by rope attached to the rock face, as were we. I felt like a bookend on the edge of a shelf.

Without opening our mouths to say another word or agree or disagree, we both checked our own and each other's harnesses and began our decent to the small clearing of moss, alpine flowers and trees in the meadow that had made such a nice place to have our picnic lunch at earlier in the day.

The moment I touched the rock on the way down I had a feeling of what was coming next. It felt cold, damp and as I looked up into the still distant sky I saw the heavy cloud the sun was pocketed in.

We both felt like we'd been beaten. A day of hard work and a cold night to look forward to as payment. It wasn't exactly my idea of a romantic night with my favourite girl.

But perhaps worse than all of this was the fact that while climbing up I didn't really need to look down and had tried to convince myself not to—climbing down was another story.

Climbing down is all about looking downward.

I decided that after tomorrow and making it up to the top, I was never going to look at another mountain again. I wasn't going to let it beat me, not on my life, but I would never again be suckered by anyone—especially myself—to be challenged to climb one again. Climbing stairs seemed plenty high.

All I wanted to do was go to sleep in my warm sleeping bag and feel the ground, firm under my feet. But it felt like I'd never get there. And the meadow, while it was flat enough and firm enough, just wasn't going to be the same—it was still up here.

# Wind

It took us a few hours to get back to the small meadow. It really was a lovely spot and after the work we'd just done to get down this far, it was the best thing I'd seen in a very long time. A thick moss grew everywhere except for a few spots where trees and small bushes broke through, it was a good place to be.

While we were smart enough to bring our sleeping bags, we didn't think we'd actually have to sleep the night out in the open so we never brought a tent. And with the wind beginning to pick up, looking into each other's eyes we knew what the other was thinking—it was going to be a very long and very cold night.

Eating the last of our food we decided to save half for tomorrow, have it for breakfast then make a break for the peak. As we ate we both nodded that we should be able to make the top by noon if we started off early and then we'd still have time to get back to the cabin and a warm, roaring fire before it was too dark.

"The moon should be a good size by tomorrow night so it'll help us out if it gets dark quick on the way down—unless you just want to hike back down tomorrow morning?"

Sarah stared at me—through me.

"Not on your life. We came to climb this rock and I'm not going down until I get up to the top."

I shrugged my shoulders, "I'm with you. I just wanted to throw out the option. I just hope we don't freeze to death tonight."

Sarah looked at me, quickly blinked and then looked back over the valley far below us from the ledge we were both sitting on, only jumping distance from a very far fall.

I tried to imagine I was sitting in a meadow in the middle of the Prairies—nice and level and as close to the ground as possible. Flat.

She looked back at me and put an arm around my shoulder. "We'll just have to keep each other warm," she smiled speaking matter of factly.

Wind whistled in my ears. I put the rest of my food into my pack and Sarah did the same, then we sat watching the sun begin to set. While I would have given my right leg to be back on the ground I couldn't think of any place on the planet I'd ever been that I saw a sunset so vast. The sky was turning the clouds red, putting a glow on the mountains around us and on our skin.

"Have I ever told you about St. Joseph—the flying saint?"

"The what?"

"The flying saint."

"I think you did mention some infatuation you had for a monk who could levitate backwards but not the flying saint...is this a joke?"

"No joke. St. Joseph, that monk you're talking about, St. Joseph of Copertino is my hero."

"I have always wanted to tell you this, but you just don't seem the kind of guy who is into all these Catholic things, flying monks, or flying saints, whatever."

"This guy is different," I moved closer to her.

"He lived in the 1600s and he flew."

"...levitated..."

"Yeah, levitated...no, flew. Anyhow, he was maybe the worst monk you could imagine—at least by the standards of the other monks—the only part of prayers or vespers he could remember was 'amen'. But even though he was so dim—or maybe because he was, he was treated like an outcast. Oh...and of course the part about him flying backwards...actually something like 70 recorded times in front of witnesses and pretty reputable ones."

Sarah was just looking at me blankly. I couldn't tell if she was interested or just interested in getting away from me.

"Is there a punchline?"

"I told you, this is no joke. This guy was the real thing." I thought back to Mel and wondered if he ever got those books back, ever finished that paper he was supposed to write. I still felt guilty for stealing from him and said a silent prayer to whatever deity might be listening that he was OK and would grow to forget he'd ever met someone low enough to rob books from him.

"If he was real then why haven't I heard of him? Why hasn't everyone—I mean shouldn't people know about a guy like this, it sounds as impressive as walking on water."

"That's a good question," I said a little unsure of a good answer myself. "Who knows, the church had no love for this guy—forbid him from going around in public, sent him away—hell, even though his flight was obviously religiously induced they put him before the Inquisition. Maybe the church just didn't want to have to answer more questions. And I mean if a dolt could be angelic or show tendencies for the divine, what would the public need to listen to priests for?"

"So I guess you're saying there was some sort of conspiracy?"

"I don't know if there is now—I mean, he's a saint so they've made him into a kind of super monk. But when he was around I'd have to say conspiracy is a good description. Kind of like the whole alien thing—everyone knows something is going on but the powers that be aren't saying a thing and would rather like the whole deal to just go away and people to forget about it and go on with their mundane, robotic lives. It's hard to control people when they suddenly have minds of their own and realize that working their whole lives for some greater good isn't what life is all about, and if a simple, stupid monk can have direct contact with a higher power what do we need churches for?"

She was hooked now like I knew she would be when she finally heard the whole story.

"So, what do you see in him?"

"I don't know. I guess I don't see just one thing that makes me aspire to learn something from his life—just everything."

I looked out over the valley, things were starting to feel like they were going silent as the sun sank lower. Sarah was deep in thought about St. Joseph or something else so I just let her relax and listen to the voices inside her head, and busied myself in getting our "bed" ready. I joined up our two sleeping bags and started throwing on the extra clothes I'd brought and motioned to Sarah to do the same.

We both knew what sleeping a night in the open in these cold, high altitude temperatures without adequate shelter could mean.

As it grew dark and we huddled together in the bag, fully clothed, the high mountain wind started picking up, whistling over the rocks and through the zippers of the bags as if they weren't even there. We giggled like small children, nervous about our situation.

"I feel kind of strange in a sleeping bag with this many clothes on—my feet tucked into my back pack with yours and cuddling my best gal for nothing more than warmth."

"So I'm your best gal?" Sarah said speaking up over the loud wind.

"Yeah, I guess you are."

Nothing more was said that night. We drifted off to sleep (if you want to call it that) with our hands warmly tucked into each other's pants to keep our fingers warm. But still we shivered and my fingers ached with cold and lack of motion.

While the howling wind blew all night there was a bizarre peacefulness about sleeping on the moss covered meadow on the side of a mountain—it sounds strange but it felt like we were both one step closer to heaven. Almost rubbing up against a divine secret.

I floated off to sleep day dreaming about being St. Joseph, lifting Sarah up into the air and back to a warm fire in front of my comfortable blue capped cabin.

# Sweet here and now

I closed my eyes in the dark and did things that no-one could ever describe as sleep. Anytime I did start to drift off, I woke back up in a shivering fit with dreams of the wind—which was literally roaring by this point—pushing us off the mossy plateau, or that the wind really was blowing millions of razor sharp needles into us, or was simply, slowly freezing us to death. But the final dream that jolted me awake for good was the most tame but terrifying of them all—Mary in a beautiful tiny house, far in the distance, but I could see her laughing in a window. I could hear the cackles echoing in the void. The joy was literally tormenting me—unable to move any closer, knowing full well she was laughing and living just fine without me, forgotten.

The rest of the night was a plague of darkness—and then the rain started to fall.

Holding each other silently shivering, our sleeping bags getting heavier and heavier with the freezing rain that was pelting us in the wind. Occasionally I could see Sarah's eyes open like mine, scanning the sky for a hint of sunlight breaking the black. We didn't talk though.

Cold can be one of the most painful things in the universe I began to realize, especially when it is mixed with a wind that feels like it is passing right through you. It numbs and stiffens. And at one point even shivering becomes painful.

And so the night dragged on. The two of us held onto each other gripping tight and thanking the creator for body warmth.

The strangest thing of living in sheer torture, as I've found out, is that after awhile, if someone were to walk up and offer to put the barrel of a gun behind your ear or beat you over the head with your own arm, it would be a deal you could take and be thankful for. There was one point in the night, after praying to God didn't seem to make a difference, I started sending out messages teasing Satan with my soul if only the morning would come.

He wasn't listening either.

The night just slowly rolled by on its own the way it always has, the only difference was that we were somewhere high above the ground in a tempest of arctic proportions.

But just as we were about to give up hope that the sun would ever show itself again, slowly and then with sudden clarity the sky lightened.

I've never been so thrilled to see anything in my whole life—seeing the sun was like seeing the face of your child peeping out between its mother's legs, that unbelievable looking-at-the-face-of-God kind of experience. I felt like a primordial man looking at that glowing orb and realizing its divine nobility.

As happens with light, in our joy the sun also gave us a glimpse of what we both looked like in this cold, damp morning. Our faces were wild with being beaten by the dark and cold, our hair soaked, near frozen, plastered to our heads.

I tried to smile but my face was too cold, skin aching as it stiffly moved. Happiness was a distant memory.

It felt strange to pull our stiff bodies out. Every muscle hurt, every joint creaked. My neck was killing me, as were my shoulders.

Sarah knelt back down to roll up the sleeping bags. Grabbing her by the shoulder I said, "I don't know about you but I don't want to haul that soaked thing up the mountain."

She looked up at me, slowly trying to process everything. It was obvious she'd had as bad a night as me. We were both so tired we moved and acted like stumbling drunken old people.

"I guess they'll be all right here—maybe they'll dry out and we can grab them on the way down."

I nodded as I turned and started to check over my pack.

We put a few rocks on the sleeping bags after opening them up to dry in the sun. After we were done we headed back up the mountain with little discussion—if for nothing else than to get our bodies moving to warm up.

Having climbed a good distance the day before and already knowing the route, the climb was a piece of cake—for the most part.

And while climbing in the early morning light wasn't exactly warm, it was warm enough—especially after the mind numbing cold of the night we'd managed to survive through. Anything a few degrees warmer was like walking through paradise.

As was the norm for us, we said little as the sun started brightening the sky and we got closer to the summit.

Soon we had climbed further than we'd gotten the day before. The top was now a lot closer than it had ever been, of course I couldn't get out of my mind that the ground was also a lot further down too.

The only drag was that with the higher altitude, or perhaps a night of less than perfect slumber, the climbing was getting a lot harder for me. But Sarah was another story—she really seemed to be in her element, she had a look in her eye and an air of madness about her. While the day before she had scrambled over boulders, today she seemed to be nearly leaping over them and up the steep face, looking back over her shoulder as if to say, "can't you do any better than that?"

A few times I just sat gasping for my breath, watching Sarah leaping her way higher, oblivious to the trouble I was having. I couldn't help but think to myself that perhaps we should be tied together again today but she seemed in another world.

I sat watching her climb when I noticed the rotting carcass of a bird squeezed between rocks beside me. I couldn't tell what kind of bird it had been, but none of that seemed to matter as I was suddenly gripped by a stomach-turning nausea. In my life I'd seen a lot of dead animals but seeing this one, which had obviously been long dead, gave me eerie flashbacks of that night seeing Ginger sprawled on the floor.

Moving some rocks over the body for one reason or another, I said a little prayer, thinking about the poor lost bird that had somehow landed here where I'd somehow landed as well. Images of birds cracking out of their shells, being fed by their mother filled my mind. I quickly wiped away a tear and took a deep breath.

"Are you coming St. Joseph? Or are you planning on sitting there all day making castles?" Sarah yelled down to me from about 100 yards ahead.

Somehow I managed to get myself up and trudge a little more up the slope.

"Sarah," I called watching her continue up towards the peak without me. I was getting seriously concerned about myself as I gasped for air and had the terrifying feelings that I was going to faint and topple backward, rolling down the mountainside.

"Sarah," I yelled again. "I have to let you know I'm dying here."

She looked back at me—my breath laboured and my legs beginning to shake from the effort of scrambling upwards for what seemed like all of time. I must have looked either pretty pathetic or plain funny—but even if I didn't, she started laughing.

"I can't believe this," she said. "We've been through all of this, survived last night, made it up this far and you're ready to run away."

"Hey, it's not my fault if I can't make it—or if it is, what do you want me to do about it?"

Sarah just stood with her arms crossed over her chest looking down at me. I felt like at any moment she was going to pick up one of the many rocks we were digging our way through, and throw it down at my head, putting me out of my misery. And with the looks she was hurtling towards me and the way I was feeling—I would have welcomed a rock upside the head.

"What?" I finally said to break the silence.

"I'm just trying to figure you out and trying to decide what I'm going to do."

"Don't you mean we?...what we're going to do?"

She looked long and hard at me, dropped her arms to her sides and said, "no, actually I mean me." She was pissed off. "Everything is always about you, isn't it?"

I just looked at her, eyes blinking a little bewildered at where exactly this was all coming from.

"I've been thinking—no, actually stewing about this—do you realize we have hardly said two words all day?"

"I did notice but I just thought we were both concentrating on what we were doing," I said, my lungs still pounding to get out of my ribcage for air.

"Ever since I first met you and before too, I'd guess, you've been solely interested in you. You decide to run away from your wife for no reason except yourself. Did whatever the hell you did in Vancouver, which you have never had the courage to tell me about. Then you ran further from whatever you're running from. You met me and basically used me for whatever turned your crank and I just went along with it all. You decide we should climb this mountain and then drag your ass and now after all this shit, you want to tell me that we're finished this climb because you're finished. Well I say fuck you!"

I didn't know quite what to say but thought I'd better say something. "Sarah, is this about me or the fact you really want to get up there?" I pointed up above us to the jagged peak that didn't look all that inviting to me any longer.

She just stood there looking at me for what felt like hours. Finally, hoisting the pack off her back and putting it at her feet, she started taking things out.

"What are you doing?"

"Making my pack lighter—you'll stay here and I'm going to the top. I imagine it'll take me about an hour at least to get up there—I'll let you know what it was like," she said putting her pack back on and marching off.

I knew better than trying to say something to talk her out of it. Instead I just sat still, watching her crawling her way up through rocks until she was completely out of view.

With an understanding someone can only have when alone on a mountain, I realized just how isolated being far above the world can really be.

I don't know how long I sat there looking at the last spot I'd seen Sarah, half expecting her to pop up on another part of the mountain or coming running and bouncing back down to get me. But she didn't.

When I really processed that she had actually gone off to finish the climb by herself I knew there was no way I'd ever know if she'd really made it or not.

And as I sat there, still trying to force air into my lungs it came with a calm certainty that there would be no way for me to know if she was alive or not. I could sit there all day waiting for her to come back not knowing if she was just taking longer than she had expected or lay dead under some rocks like the corpse of the discarded bird I'd found.

Pacing around on the thin ridge of rock we'd been venturing up, I nervously kept flashing my eyes to the peak above.

Although I knew better I couldn't help but sneak a look into the void on the other side of the ridge. Somewhere down there was my cabin—you couldn't even see the highway from this height. Everything was different. And with the change in weather, with fog and clouds rolling in below me, the ground was more fuzzy grey thing than the lush green I'd seen before. Standing up on the ledge looking down made me feel like I was the last person alive on the planet, looking deep into the bottomless pit that used to be the Earth.

A few times I could swear I heard voices calling me—not Sarah's, but someone's. First I heard a woman's voice that sounded similar to Mary, then another like my long dead mother—then a chorus of voices all strangely familiar but just out of ear shot. I was thankful I couldn't make out what they were saying, and instead just told myself the elevation and my isolation were ganging up on my mind.

I sat down where I stood, feet dangling over the maw.

Like a child waking from a nightmare I closed my eyes. I knew it was the altitude and my nerves that were causing the voices and my anxiety. I couldn't help but remember childhood night terrors that would wake me, drenched in sweat, rocking back and forth, ears covered to silence the sound of nothing—clocks ticking, the sink dripping, and the drawing of breath.

Holding my head, feeling veins pulse I looked up at the peak standing phallic, silently at attention. Talking to myself I prayed Sarah would show herself, waving from a ledge. I wanted to be with her or have her here. I wanted to hold someone, tell them how sorry I was for all the stupidity of my life.

Looking at my arms I rolled up the sleeves looking for some telltale mark of my addiction but the scars were long healed. I looked up at the sky and said to a passing cloud that I was sorry.

The silence around me was suffocating, cloying.

"Sarah!" I yelled, hearing her name bouncing off the rocks, rolling back to me over and over again.

My legs started shaking violently, jerking my feet in the open air above the drop where I sat. Looking past my feet I could see a bird circling somewhere down below.

With eyes closed I turned my head back the way Sarah had gone and let out another cry. "Sarah...if you hear me shout back."

Nothing.

"She's totally right," I said opening my eyes again, looking at the open air beneath my feet. "She's totally right—it is about me. God forgive me if my stupidity has hurt her like it has already hurt Mary. Sarah shouldn't be up there alone."

Images of all the people, some nameless, others that I'd known in my life danced before my eyes in the open air, just out of reach.

The voices again.

I felt the cold wind on my face, the frigid rock under my legs and knew with a calm serenity that life may well be suffering but we all have a chance to make it better or worse. So far I'd aspired to make my life and everyone else's life special but in reality had only made a mess of things. I knew this as certainly as I knew I was sitting far too close to the edge.

Still no sign of her. Sarah shouldn't be alone up there—if I had to crawl all the way to the top I'd do it—and gladly, just to know she was all right.

"Things are going to be different," I said aloud. "I may not be the climber I thought I was but coming up here has given me something way better than I'd ever get by just reaching the peak."

Hoisting my legs up and under me I reached out for a hand-sized rock outcropping, sitting perfectly within my reach offering itself to help me get up.

As I smiled once again about the synchronicity of there seeming to always be a handhold only an arm's length away, I felt the muscles in my arm pulling me up—it was a millisecond later that the rock broke free.

I watched in a strange slow motion as I felt myself coming loose from the ridge, tumbling backwards into nothing, the hand-sized rock still gripped firmly in my hand. It was as if I was watching myself fall and falling, both at the same time.

I'm not quite sure if it took a second or milliseconds to realize I was falling backwards into the same darkening nothing I'd only a minute before been gazing into. But it hit like a rock falling from the sky.

For what seemed like an eternity, I watched the peak of the mountain falling further and further out of grasp. For a brief moment I was certain I could see a lone figure straddling the topmost point of the mountain, wide-eyed, waving.

I wondered with sombre stillness if there was any truth to what people say about those who fall from great distances, dying of shock before they ever hit the ground, hoping it was true.

As I fell the wind whistling in my ears was deafening, I could see my hair waving like  streamers—my clothes were making a familiar fluttering sound I remember from childhood when my mother would hang clothes on the line in a strong wind to dry them out.

I looked to my side and thought I could just make out the blue tarp of my cabin in the woods.

I closed my eyes and saw the face of Mary—she was smiling. In my mind I reached out to her, feeling her soft skin. I could smell the familiar scent of her hair. "I'm sorry Mary…"

Forcing my eyes open I looked into the dark sky and wondered if this was what St. Joseph had felt like, flying backwards into the void. But I knew there was a big difference between him levitating and me simply falling.

The cold wind was ripping tears from my eyes.

My life didn't flash before me like people always talk about in moments like these. Time however, did seem to be slowing—either that or we really had climbed further than I'd thought. Not that it mattered at this point, but I could see clearly and understood that life really was like the snapping of fingers and all between birth and death just illusion, distracting us from the simple truth that this is all we have. Now is all there is. What matters isn't what we do but how we do it.

But I knew this before—I'd heard the words before—only now it was all different. It's like driving, you can understand how it works but until you actually get behind the wheel everything is different.

As I looked to my side, wind whistling in my ears I didn't have to tell myself that it was too late for me. I'd spent too much time fighting the moment, spent too much time looking, a lifetime of running, of fleeing and not enough time just sitting, just breathing, just smiling.

I closed my eyes again realizing the ground was rising up to swallow me, choosing to enter into the bright light of the other side without seeing that massive piece of rock falling away from me.

Saying a silent prayer of thanks I apologized to God for not having lived the life I should have, "…please take care of Mary and Sarah…I'm sorry I wasn't a better person…I wish I could have lived the life I'd set out to…I understand things much better now…all I wanted was to live a good life, be a good person. I miss so much, so many people..."

From somewhere deep in the backs of my eyes a light began shining outwards and I felt suddenly like I was no longer falling but floating.

I opened my eyes and realized that not only was I not falling but I was no longer moving at all. The canopy of trees lay around me in all directions—maybe 50 feet below me—the rock of the mountain stood in front of me unchanging.

"Sometimes we must fall a far way before we realize that it is time to get back up and move on," a calm, gentle voice said from below. Turning my head I saw I was somehow in the arms of a smiling man in the robes of a Christian monk—he too was just floating.

I closed my eyes slowly like I'd just stood up and banged by head into something that I could have sworn was much further away. I started opening my mouth to say something but no words would come out and then before I could process the current situation more fully I realized I was flying upwards at an incredible speed.

Before I had time to look back down at this strangely floating man, his arms were putting me back where I'd sat only moments before, as gently as a father putting a sleeping four-year-old to bed.

I blinked again.

Sitting on the cold rock I looked beneath the feet of the robed figure into the void—nothing. I don't know what I expected to find, strings, a ladder or wings, but there was nothing, only two bare feet hardly moving under a brown robe.

I opened my mouth to talk again.

The figure smiled down at me, opened its arms, palms towards me.

With a calm clarity I realized this bizarre hovering being was none other than St. Joseph. I didn't have to ask. I didn't have to be told. I just knew from the very core of my being.

He smiled at me somehow knowing I was beginning to get it—finally.

I smiled back.

In a flash he moved back from the mountain 50 feet seeming somehow to be even more out in mid-air. A cold wind blew. I could smell roses, as if they were surrounding me.

From out of every pour of his body a light started to seep, slowly at first and then so fast that the once plain, brown robed monk was now enveloped in a pulsating white-gold light. Not a light like turning on a switch but a light like you saw as a child staring into the glowing embers of a campfire when everyone else had gone to bed. I was transfixed, warm and in a space in time beyond description.

With the light increasing, slowly as if spinning like a dervish the smiling face turned, changed from St. Joseph to that of Buddha, then slowly to Jesus, Krishna, Moses, the Virgin Mary, the Dalai Lama, and others I couldn't recognize. I sat there unable to move, mouth hanging open, eyes wide, glaring.

Finally the transformation stopped. Still sitting on the ledge I looked eye to eye with an image of myself floating above that open wound between mountains.

I smiled, bowed my head and closed my eyes to the increasing glow.

# End

I'm not sure how long I sat there like that, but when I finally did look back up my strange visitor had vanished.

Without a second thought or a wonder at what had just transpired I scrambled backwards this time not planning on reaching for any outcropping that "looked just right" and stood back a body's length from the edge. I looked out into the open space and took a deep breath hoping to get a whiff of the roses I'd smelled earlier but as happens with all things, their time had come and gone.

Glancing up towards the peak of the mountain I looked briefly for Sarah moving amid the rocks. Nothing. But strangely I knew she was all right—we'd all be all right, we just needed a little courage and a little faith.

Turning my back on the mountain and the past, I reached down for my pack, throwing it on with a chuckle, feeling like Hotei or Santa Claus but more than all of that, feeling like myself for the first time in my life.

Without another thought of what treasure may lay hidden at the top of this granite peak or any other, I headed back down to the rest of the world.